Sheltering Reagan

Mountain Mastery Series

By
Avery Gale

© Copyright August 2017 by Avery Gale
ISBN 978-1-944472-41-2
All cover art and logo © Copyright 2017 by Avery Gale
All rights reserved.

Mountain Mastery® and Avery Gale® are registered trademarks
Published by Avery Gale Books

Thank you for respecting the hard work of this author.

This is a work of fiction. Names, places, characters and incidents either are the product of the author's imagination or are used fictitiously and any resemblance to any actual persons, living or dead, organizations, events or locales are entirely coincidental.

No part of this book may be reproduced, stored in a retrieval system, or transmitted by any means without the written permission of the author and publishing company.

WARNING: The unauthorized reproduction or distribution of this copyrighted work is illegal. Criminal copyright infringement, including infringement without monetary gain, is investigated by the FBI and is punishable by up to 5 years in federal prison and a fine of $250,000.

Prologue

PLEASURE. NOTHING BUT mind-numbing pleasure. Reagan moaned when she felt the smooth sheet beneath her. The fabric slid against her bare back in a sensual caress...a cool contrast to the heat pressing against her chest and lower abdomen. Hot skin and the rasp of soft hair arrowing down to a taut abdomen blanketed her in warmth. Fucking hell, the ridges of his six-pack sent sparks of electricity straight to her sex.

Her nipples were hypersensitive, the faintest brush of air making her empty pussy clench in need. The clips pinching her nipples made them throb in time with every beat of her heart. The silky hair on his legs rubbed against the inside of Reagan's thighs, as he pushed them farther apart. With her arms bound to the headboard, she couldn't do anything to alleviate the pressure growing inside her, and it grew exponentially with every breath she took.

Calloused fingers moved over her ribs, tracing a path down her torso until they bracketed her hips. The feeling of being restrained made her breath catch as goose bumps raced over her fiery skin. "Like being restrained, do you? I will test that, Reagan. Tying you down and pushing your limits will be my greatest pleasure."

When she didn't respond, he tightened his grip. The hold might have seemed punishing if she hadn't wanted him so badly she could barely think. "What do you want, Reagan? Tell me." This wasn't a rhetorical question. He expected an answer.

Tell him? Was he serious? Reagan wanted to feel him slide his cock into her wet sheath, the ridges and veins lighting up each and every nerve ending. She panted, her breaths coming so fast and shallow she worried she might hyperventilate. And with blood pooling in her breasts and sex, there wasn't enough to feed the part of her brain responsible for coherent speech. He expected an answer, but she wasn't sure her brain was getting enough oxygen to work properly.

"More." She was elated she'd been able to string enough letters together to form a real word.

"More what? More of this?" His tongue lashed her left nipple, making her moan in response. "No? Then perhaps more of this?" He moved up to seal his lips over hers, his tongue ravaging her mouth, leaving no part untouched. This wasn't a kiss of seduction; this was a claiming, and it sent her spiraling closer to release. By the time he pulled back, Reagan's head was swimming. Damn, the man could make her come just by kissing her.

Even though she couldn't see his face, she felt to her bones who was shifting lower, wedging his cock at her entrance. The smooth head was flame hot, and she squirmed in a futile attempt to press herself onto his length. The man chuckled, and the vibrations ignited every cell in her body. "Please." Reagan wasn't sure what she was begging for, but he seemed to understand what she hadn't been able to put into words.

"How can I say no when you ask so sweetly?" With a swivel of his hips, he pushed in far enough to make her gasp at the sudden stretch of her swollen tissues. The burn was exquisite, and she tried unsuccessfully to tilt her hips up and force him deeper. "So very greedy. I knew you'd be perfect. Your body responds perfectly to my touch; it knows we were matched by the heavens.

"Mine." His voice was gruff...his own desire challenging the usual smoky tone as he growled the word against her ear. The resonating timbre ratcheted her desire higher each time he made love to her. "Say it. Say you are mine."

"Yes. Yours." And she was. Everything in her realized the truth. As soon as the words crossed her lips, he thrust into her depths. The scorching stretch launched her over the edge straight into a blinding orgasm where brilliant white lights singed the insides of her eyelids. Every muscle in her body contracted as electricity blazed over nerve endings like lightning. She smothered her scream against his shoulder, but his continued thrusts were stealing her ability to think.

The sound of his harsh breathing against her ear, the sweet words of encouragement, and the soul stealing orgasm she could feel building in her core were too much to assimilate. "You belong to me. Don't ever doubt that. You are mine, Peach."

The minute he called her by the sweet nickname he'd given her, Reagan came awake with a start.

Sitting up in bed, she clutched the sheet to her chest. She gasped for breath as her mind slowly surfaced from the fog of the dream and drifted back from the edge of the release she'd been so close to. Dammit to all. Holy fucking fudge, she'd wanted that second orgasm. Her body was practically vibrating off the bed with the need to find the relief she'd been so close to.

She'd had the same dream for the past several nights, each one progressing further into intimacy they shared. What did it mean that she was suddenly dreaming about the man she'd been watching for several months?

Looking at her bedside clock, Reagan sighed in defeat. She needed to get up and take another shower. Maybe she could wash away the memory of how his hands felt as they skimmed over her bare flesh. Hopefully, the scent of her body shampoo would wash away the lingering scent of his musk from her memory. She was embarrassingly wet, but the feeling that she'd been denied something special taunted her as she shivered in the cold room.

While she waited for the water to warm up, Reagan sent a quick text to Kelsey asking for a ride. If she had to shower in a sixty-degree bathroom, she needed the water as warm as possible. Since her co-worker had to drive by Reagan's apartment, she didn't ordinarily mind stopping. Promising to be waiting outside in fifteen minutes, Reagan finished her shower in record time. There wasn't enough time to dry her hair. She'd be lucky if she didn't catch her death standing on the curb this early in the morning in the flimsy jacket she called a coat.

Rushing out the door, she wondered what the dreams meant. Rafe Newell had barely spoken to her beyond polite greetings and telling her she smelled like peaches. Pushing the questions to the back of her mind, Reagan climbed into Kelsey's warm car and settled in to listen to the other woman recount all the intimate details of the date she'd had the previous night. The woman had no filters. Reagan wished her own car wasn't on the fritz again, but wishes didn't change facts, and they damned well didn't pay the bills.

Chapter One

REAGAN WALSH BIT her bottom lip as she watched Rafe Newell's long legs eat up the distance as he crossed the tarmac. It should be a crime for any man to be so good looking. Six plus feet of pure dominant male. His dark hair looked like it was a couple of weeks past a scheduled trim, the soft waves curling at the collar of his white linen shirt. With his tie loosened and suit jacket slung over his shoulder, his sauntering gait made him appear more like a GQ model than a world-renowned plastic surgeon.

"You're drooling, Reagan." Kelsey Jones was the first person Reagan met when she moved to Montana. Over time, they'd become friends because they spent so many hours together at work. The two of them usually spent their lunch breaks dreaming about finding better jobs, but there didn't seem to be much on the horizon for either of them.

Reagan kept hearing rumors the small regional air carrier they worked for planned to merge with a larger company on the west coast, but her boss hadn't confirmed or denied the chatter. Being the paranoid person she was, Reagan had recently accepted a part-time waitressing job at a nearby kink club. She'd nearly tripped over her own feet the first night when she'd seen the man who starred in all her sexual fantasies walk into the club's opulent main room.

"I am not drooling." She caught herself before she could smooth her fingers over her mouth to check, a move she was certain would earn her a bark of laughter and weeks of relentless teasing from her friend. "Oh my God, he's coming in." In all the months she'd been watching him, he'd never deviated from his set path. Pilot Rafe had proven to be as predictable as Master Rafe was unpredictable.

"Places to go, people to see. I'm outta here. Have fun and don't do anything I wouldn't do." Kelsey's sing-song voice was tinged with something other than fun as it faded into the back room. Reagan was alone when Rafe pushed open the glass door of the cargo company's small office, and she could have sworn all the air was suddenly sucked out of the room, leaving her gasping for oxygen.

He's probably lost. Don't panic. And for fucksake don't babble. Reagan forced a smile in greeting and sent up a silent prayer Kelsey had been kidding about the drool.

"Good afternoon, Reagan." His deep voice sent shock waves of need all the way to her core.

"Dr. Newell, h-hi. W-what can I do for you?" Damn her nervous stutter.

His panty-dropping smile sent a surge of heat searing through her, and she felt her cheeks flame. "Are you working at the club this evening?"

Landon and Savannah Nixon had gotten married a few days earlier and were celebrating this evening with a reception at Mountain Mastery. Reagan had been asked to serve during the last half of the party and to help the caterers clean up since she was familiar with where things belonged in the club's enormous storage room.

"Yes, Sir." His eyes widened, and she saw heat flash in

them before it was masked behind his usual cool, indifferent expression.

"Very good, Peach." His smooth voice flowed over her like warm honey, and Reagan felt the warmth all the way to her toes.

He'd given her the nickname the first night she'd worked at the club. She'd leaned close, trying to clean up a spilled drink, and inadvertently sent her long chestnut hair tumbling over his bare arm. He'd wrapped the waist length strands around his hand and tugged her closer enough he could bury his nose in the silky locks. Whispering against her ear, Master Rafe had told her, "You smell like peaches. Are you as sweet and juicy as a ripe peach, Reagan?" His question had shocked her, but she hadn't gotten an opportunity to answer. Master Nate's admonishment that she was working caused Rafe to release her, but not before he'd ignited something deep inside her. Reagan's knees had been quaking so violently she'd worried her legs wouldn't hold her up.

"Reagan?" His use of her real name startled her out of the foray she'd taken into the memory. Damn, had he asked her a question? "Where were you?"

"Where?"

"Don't play coy, Peach. I spoke to you twice before you responded. Tell me what was so enchanting it changed your respiration rate and dilated those pretty brown eyes."

"Peaches. Umm, I was just remembering my first night at the club. You said I smelled like peaches." He didn't respond, but his lips twitched in amusement. "I'm sorry. Did you want me to do something for you this evening?"

The minute the words slipped past her lips, Reagan was certain she'd made a mistake. The blatant sexual innuendo mortified her. Covering her face with her hands, she shook her head. "Oh, God. I swear I didn't mean that the way it sounded."

"Hmmm? Pity." She didn't need to see his face to know he was amused. She could practically hear the laughter in his voice. Sucking in a deep breath, she put her hands back on the counter. "What time do you get off work?"

Reagan glanced at her watch before answering. "In fifteen minutes. I'm the last one here, so I will begin locking up in a few minutes. Did you need something, Sir?"

"Do you have plans for dinner?"

"D-dinner?" God bless it, she sounded like a stammering fool. And everything about Rafe Newell made her as jumpy as frog legs in a hot skillet.

"Yes, the meal one usually eats in the evening?" He grinned at her, and she felt her cheeks flame again. Using the backs of his fingers, he brushed over the hot flesh. "You flush such a beautiful shade of red. I wonder what other parts of you I could turn that lovely hue?"

She glanced down at the ugly khaki uniform shirt she wore with her well-worn jeans and sighed. "I'm not really dressed to go out." It wouldn't matter if she had time to go home and change since she didn't have anything remotely nice enough for a dinner date. At one time, she'd had a closet full of beautiful clothes. But those, along with the shoes and jewelry she'd sold, were all part of the price she'd paid for her escape.

When she looked up, he was studying her closely. "I'm interested in the person beneath the clothing, Peach. Did you drive to work?"

"No, Sir. I rode with Kelsey." *And she bolted when she saw you headed this way.*

"And where is Kelsey now?" The small lines between his brows were the only indication he wasn't pleased.

"Umm, she had to leave, I guess." Reagan wasn't going to tell him the other woman had laughed at her more than once for staring as he'd walked by. Kelsey had a way of making Reagan feel like a girl from the wrong side of the tracks watching a party from afar.

"And she left you here alone without a ride?" When she didn't respond, he shook his head. "Sweetheart, I do believe you need to reevaluate your dependence on co-workers for rides. How would you have gotten home?"

"It's only a few miles. I usually walk to the bus stop and then…" She didn't finish because she could have sworn she heard him growl.

"Lock up and let's go get something to eat. Then I'll take you to your place so you can get whatever you need for work."

RAFE REINED IN his growing frustration. Didn't it figure that the day he'd finally decided to ask Reagan to dinner, she'd be talking to the one woman he made every effort to avoid? He'd had a clear view into the office as he walked across the small airport's open tarmac and seen the two women standing at the counter. Reagan's attention had been focused on him, her expression a perfect mixture of desire and apprehension. He doubted she understood what a siren's call that combination was to a man as sexually dominant as Rafe.

His reputation as a sadist had been exaggerated by the club's rabid rumor mill, but it wasn't entirely without merit. Most sadists gained their sexual pleasure from causing pain; Rafe's came from pushing a submissive's boundaries until they were a heartbeat from snapping. He wanted subs to experience the blurring of the line between pleasure and pain. Gaining a submissive's trust—having her surrender her body into his care—was a heady feeling. The significance of that gift couldn't be overstated.

Sending a willing submissive into sub-space was the goal of every scene. The subs he played with understood what he expected. They were also certain he'd go to the mat to take them to entirely new levels of sexual satisfaction. Opening a sub's eyes to higher, more intense levels of pleasure would put a smile on any Dom's face. But one of the first things newbie subs discovered was that he only played at the club. He didn't date club members—ever.

Rafe had the feeling Reagan Walsh was going to be an exception to every rule. She'd caught his eye months ago when he'd walked by as she was washing the wall of windows at the front of the local airports only cargo carrier. She'd been watching him in the glass reflection, and when he'd spoken to her as he passed, she'd smiled sweetly and nodded in response. He had gotten the impression she was shy rather than unfriendly; something about her intrigued him. The next week, he'd made a point to fly in at approximately the same time, hoping to see her again. They'd repeated the same dance of distance for two more weeks before he'd shown up an hour late one Thursday and missed her.

Cursing his scatterbrained assistant for overscheduling him before a three-day weekend, Rafe had been in such a foul mood he'd almost re-boarded his jet and returned to San Francisco. One of the perks of flying himself was being able to leave as soon as the ground crew finished refueling. But his co-pilot was already glued to his date in a lip-lock Rafe worried might melt the asphalt from the parking lot.

Muttering under his breath, Rafe decided there was no reason to spoil their fun just because he'd missed saying hello to a woman he still hadn't had the courage to talk to.

Thank God he hadn't given in to his temper because what he'd found when he walked into Mountain Mastery's main room later that evening had been a game changer. Two steps beyond the door, his gaze landed on the woman who was starring in all his fantasies without ever saying more than "good afternoon." Watching her move around the room while serving drinks, he noted the economy of her movements. Even her smallest moves had purpose; nothing was wasted effort. It was mesmerizing to watch.

Bringing his thoughts back to the present, Rafe hadn't been surprised when he saw Kelsey scurry out the back door of the small cargo carrier's office. The damned woman was a menace. It was unfortunate she and Reagan appeared to be friendly. He made a mental note to ask Nate if the other woman was still a member of the club. It had been months since he'd seen her around, but that didn't mean she wasn't simply avoiding him. *I should be so lucky.*

He'd played with Kelsey twice at the club, but she hadn't been pleased when he'd refused to fuck her. If he'd listened to his inner voice, he'd have never agreed to the second scene. But he'd been bored, and she'd been available. *She's also bat-shit crazy.* She'd rocketed from begging and contrite to psychotic stalker in the time it had taken him fly back to San Francisco. Getting rid of her had taken law enforcement intervention, and the price of her return ticket to Montana had been money well spent.

Typical Kelsey—the world revolved around her. She'd left her friend to find her own way home, and on a night when Reagan had to work, too. Watching Reagan move around the small office, checking to be sure everything was secured, was enlightening. He couldn't hold back his smile when she nervously checked the same door for the third time. "Do I make you uncomfortable, Peach?"

"Yes. Sir. Dr. Newell." Her face was crimson by the time she stopped trying to determine exactly how she should address him.

"We aren't playing, so please call me Rafe. I'm guessing you don't usually address your dinner companions so formally." She stared at him, blinking several times as if that was going to clear up what he'd said. He waited until he saw the corners of her mouth twitch as she tried to hold back her grin.

"I'm sure you would be right…*if* I had dinner companions. As it is, I usually miss dinner." He could tell she'd revealed more than she'd intended to, but he held his questions. There would be plenty of time to make inquiries later. Rafe held the door open and watched her pull the lightweight jacket she was wearing around her. He'd barely landed ahead of the storm front moving through, and the temperature was plummeting fast.

Wrapping his suit jacket around her, Rafe led Reagan to his SUV. He settled her into the plush leather seat and leaned close to fasten her seat belt. The soft scent of peaches was tempting, but she wasn't ready for him to taste her the way he wanted to. "You've worked all day and still smell like peaches." He pressed a quick kiss to her forehead then added, "Sit tight. I'll get the car warmed up so you stop shivering." He cursed Kelsey again as he rounded the front of his SUV. Reagan would have been frozen by the time she walked to the bus stop.

During the short drive into town, he noticed her fidgeting in her seat. "Spit it out, Peach. What's on your mind?"

"I just wanted to say thanks. It would have been a *really* cold walk. Working two jobs doesn't leave me a lot of time to go shopping for a warmer coat."

"You don't have anything else?" When she shook her head, his hands tightened around the steering wheel. "I'm assuming you moved from a much warmer climate, because that light weight jacket is not going to get you through the winter, sweetheart." Hell, it wasn't enough now. "Why *are* you working two jobs?"

He noticed her stiffen, but she answered without hesitating. "There are rumors the cargo company is going to lay off a couple people. I'm already barely getting by, and losing that income would put me out on the street. Since I haven't been there long, I'll be one of the first to go. So, it seemed smart to try to save enough money to tide me over."

Rafe wondered how she'd ended up in Montana, but didn't want to steer the conversation in a different direction. "I'd heard they were being bought out, but I hadn't heard they planned to pare down their employee roster."

When he'd first noticed Reagan, he asked a few of the other pilots about the company she worked for. The small airport was almost a community itself, so one question had brought a torrent of information. No one had mentioned layoffs, but he could see why she was concerned. Rafe was damned impressed she was willing to work hard to give herself a financial cushion.

Parking in front of a small café, Rafe turned in his seat so he could look at the beautiful woman sitting beside him. "This place has great food. Have you eaten here?"

"No. I don't eat out very often because it's too expensive."

"What did you eat for dinner last night, Reagan?" He'd

tried to keep his voice neutral, but was convinced he hadn't succeeded when he saw her barely perceptible flinch. Rafe thought for a minute she might lie to him, but when her shoulders sagged, he didn't doubt he'd get the truth.

"I had the second half of my Ramen noodle burrito."

"Breakfast?" She shook her head. He got the same response when he asked about lunch. Closing his eyes, Rafe shook his head and cursed under his breath. "Stay right where you are, Peach." He stalked around the SUV and was pleased she hadn't made any effort to get out on her own. Helping her to her feet, he tucked her hand into the crook of his arm and led her into the quaint eatery. The floors were covered in tile squares so well-worn the speckles had long since faded from the surface. The countertops and tables still sported Formica® Rafe assumed was original in the 1950s.

Reagan drew in a deep breath as she seemed to be absorbing the ambiance surrounding her. A sensual smile slowly curved her lips, and Rafe's heart skipped a beat. *She has no idea how beautiful she is, and that makes her even more attractive.*

Chapter Two

REAGAN DIDN'T REMEMBER the last time she'd eaten anything as delicious as the meal Rafe ordered when she'd been unable to decide. After her stomach growled so loud he'd heard it across the table, Rafe had shaken his head and given the middle-aged waitress their meal selections. "Peach, I don't usually order for my dinner dates without asking first. But it seemed as though your inability to make a decision might well lead to starvation, and that wasn't going to do a thing for my reputation."

She'd laughed at his faux concern for the damage her collapse would do to his standing in the kink community. "I haven't worked at the club long, but it does seem they might frown on a Dom having a woman expire on their watch. And since you're a physician, I doubt your colleagues would be very understanding, either. Heaven knows hospitals are a terrible place to keep anything under wraps."

Dropping her gaze to the table, Reagan hoped he didn't ask her how she'd learned about the rumor mills operating inside most medical facilities. She'd almost laughed out loud when Master Nate warned her about the subversive chatter he called a common curse in BDSM clubs. Since she'd been completely transparent with them, he'd quickly realized the irony of his comments. Considering her personal background, his cautionary words were unnecessary.

"Reagan?"

The sound of Rafe's voice brought her back to the moment, and she wondered for a moment how long he'd been speaking to her. *Cripes, inattention almost got me killed a year ago. You'd think I'd have learned my lesson.*

"I'm sorry. Guess I'm a bit more spent than I realized." She might not sleep enough, but the extra money would go a long way to ensuring she wasn't out on the street if she got laid off.

Small frown lines formed between his brows. "How long are you planning to work both jobs?"

"As long as I can. Savings accounts drain pretty quickly when you are unemployed." Reagan was grateful she was saved from the questions she saw in his eyes when the waitress appeared with their food. Rafe didn't look pleased with the waitress's timing, but since they'd already established this was the first meal she'd have today, he didn't protest. It was probably a short reprieve, but Regan held out hope she could redirect the conversation.

They finished their meals with minimal conversation, and when she finally glanced up from her empty plate, Rafe was smiling at her. His expression was more amused indulgence than judgement, but that didn't keep her embarrassment from stealing her breath. Reagan felt her cheeks flush, but he shook his head. "Don't. I'm thrilled you enjoyed your dinner."

She relaxed and shook her head. "It was delicious. For a small diner, the food is amazing." She leaned back and sighed. "Hopefully, this will reenergize me." Glancing at her watch, Reagan grimaced. "I hate to be a killjoy, but I need to get home and change." It wouldn't take her long to walk to the bus stop, but the route ended almost a mile from the club, so she needed to allow extra time to cover the distance.

"Come." He stood and held out his hand. Rafe pulled her slowly to her feet and then settled his warm palm against her lower back as they walked out. She couldn't hold back the shiver that moved through her at the possessive heat of his hand through her thin shirt.

After he'd settled her in his luxury SUV, Reagan realized she was going to have to tell him where she lived. Dreading his response to her living accommodations, she considered giving him a phony address. But, since she was probably the worst liar in the history of the world, she quickly discounted the idea. *Why am I trying to impress a man who is going to walk away as soon as he sees my scars?* Of all the men in the world who wouldn't want to be seen with her, a renowned plastic surgeon was at the top of the list.

RAFE WATCHED REAGAN'S hands twist in her lap as they neared the address she'd given him. Nothing about her added up. During their conversation at dinner, she'd been articulate and insightful, even giving him some great suggestions about possible locations when he'd mentioned considering moving his practice from San Francisco. She'd given compelling arguments for the need for patient care in both Texas and Montana. She had a clear command of the terminology, making him wonder if she had a medical background.

He'd parked in front of her small apartment, but he

wasn't looking at the ancient building's crumbling façade. His attention was focused on the nervous woman sitting beside him. Reaching for the door handle, Rafe watched Reagan paste a fake smile on her face before turning to him. *Oh, little sub, you have so much to learn about Doms. Reading body language is what we do, darling.* "Well, thanks so much for dinner and the ride home. I'll...well, I guess I will see you later."

"Take your hand off the handle, Reagan." His tone made it clear the words had been a command, and her hand rested back in her lap before she'd even registered what he'd said. "Good girl. When you are with me, I'll always open doors for you. I'm going to walk you in and wait until you're ready to go to the club."

"YOU DON'T HAVE to do that, Sir." Damn. Even she'd been able to hear how unconvincing she'd sounded. His tight smile didn't reach his eyes, nor did he bother to respond before getting out of the SUV.

He moved around the front of his vehicle, and she felt a burst of heat rocket from her core. Dr. Rafe Newell had to be the sexiest man she'd ever met. Everything about him flipped her switches. She'd seen him shirtless with his leathers riding low on his hips at the club one night and almost tripped over her own tongue. The image was still burned into her brain and fueling her darkest fantasies.

"Come. Let's get you inside where it's warmer." She'd been so lost in thought she hadn't even realized he'd opened her door. His deep voice would have made her swoon, but suddenly, all she could think about was what he was going to be say when he stepped into her apartment. Two minutes later, she had her answer. "It's fucking freezing in here."

"The landlord hasn't had time to fix the furnace. I'm sure he'll get to it soon." *At least I hope to hell he does, because showers are pure torture.*

"The temperature is going to drop dramatically during the next few hours, Peach. It will be impossible for you to sleep here. How are you supposed to even shower? Good God, it can't be more than fifty fucking degrees in here."

He pushed his hand through his hair in frustration as he looked around at her humble abode. "Listen, I have a house close by. There are several spare bedrooms, and it's warm." He returned his focus to her, drilling her with a stare so intense it felt like he was touching her. She didn't move. She was afraid to breath. "Do you trust me, Reagan?"

"Yes, Sir." The words slipped out so easily Reagan realized they were true. She shouldn't. Watching someone for several weeks wasn't the same as *knowing* them.

"Put a few things together, and we'll be on our way. We'll come back in the morning to be sure the heat is on." She could see the muscles in his jaw ticking. He was obviously barely holding his temper in check.

Gathering what she'd need for the night, she didn't waste any time and could tell he was surprised when she announced she was ready. "Before we go…I'd like…well, I want to say thanks. I wasn't looking forward to taking a shower here."

Rafe's entire demeanor softened. "You're most welcome, Reagan. I'm grateful you didn't protest. I'm not sure I'd have been able to leave you here later tonight." She appreciated his concern. It had been a while since she'd had someone to worry about her. Heaven knew the staff at the prison where she'd volunteered hadn't given her safety a second thought. Shuddering as memories started to assail her, Reagan felt Rafe's arm encircle her shoulders. "Come on. Let's go. It's too cold in here for you. Please tell me you have something warmer to wear."

Pulling a slightly heavier jacket from a peg near the door, she grinned. "I know it isn't much, but I didn't need anything warmer before I moved to Montana. I just haven't had the time or been willing to part with the money to buy a heavy coat yet." She'd been more worried about being able to keep a roof over her head than buying a parka, but even she was willing to admit it was time to find something more substantial.

He helped her into the lightweight coat while muttering something about shopping never being a problem for any other women he'd known. She almost laughed at his bewildered musing. Even before she'd been attacked, she hadn't particularly enjoyed shopping for clothes. And now it was even worse. Seeing the horror on a sales clerk's face when she'd stepped into the dressing room unannounced was an experience Reagan wasn't anxious to repeat. The older woman hadn't intended to hurt Reagan's feelings, and she'd shuttered her horror quickly, but not before Reagan saw the shock in her eyes. Reagan didn't need the reminder of the scars she carried. *Yeah, I have to look at them every day.*

RAFE CHUCKLED WHEN he helped Reagan from the car, and she gasped. "Holy hell, it's warmer in your garage than it was my apartment. That's just wrong." He didn't remind her the door had just been wide open, also. It would have been practically balmy inside a few moments earlier.

Keying in his security code, he opened the door and led her into the kitchen. He'd already turned the heat up via the app on his phone. His hand tightened around her upper arm when she stopped suddenly. "What's wrong, Peach?"

"It's beautiful. Your home, I mean." Her eyes were wide as they surveyed the large chef's kitchen. "And if you don't live here full-time...I have to wonder what your home in San Francisco must look like."

Chuckling, Rafe let his hand slide down her arm so he could link his fingers with hers. "Come on, sweetness. Would you like something to drink?"

"A cup of coffee would be wonderful. I have a feeling I'm going to need the caffeine tonight. I have the second shift, but clean-up can take a while after special events." He fixed her a small cup of coffee and smiled at her frustrated grumbling.

"Caffeine isn't the answer, Peach." Taking her small hand in his, he led her down the hall to the largest of the guest rooms. "I think you'll find everything you need in the attached bath, but if there's something else that will make you feel at home, just let me know." It wasn't easy to walk away, but he forced himself to step out of the room before he pushed her against the wall and kissed her senseless. Reagan Walsh was temptation personified. Only time would tell if the two of them would be compatible in the playroom, but for the first time in years, he was anxious to learn more about a woman than how many ways he could make her come.

Making his way quickly to the other side of the house, Rafe pulled his phone from his pocket and dialed Nate

Ledek. As one of the owners of the Mountain Mastery Club, he would have interviewed Reagan when she applied for the job. After Rafe explained the situation with Reagan's apartment, Nate snarled a string of expletives. "I can tell you from experience the man she's dealing with is anything but honest. There probably isn't a damned thing wrong with the furnace. He'll set it just high enough to keep the pipes from freezing until she threatens to move."

Rafe wasn't surprised. He hated landlords who took advantage of their tenants, particularly when it was a single woman living alone. "I'll pay him a visit tomorrow. Hopefully, he'll fix it."

"It'll probably take you a couple of weeks to track him down. He runs everything remotely and is rarely in Montana. I'm not sure I can help her find another rental at this time of year. The skiers have probably snagged everything by now." Nate sounded as frustrated as Rafe felt.

They talked briefly about her housing options before Nate asked the question Rafe had been certain the club owner would voice. "Is your interest personal or professional?"

"There is nothing professional about my interest in Reagan. Why would there be?"

"We'll talk when you get here. There are things you need to know. I didn't realize you were interested in her, or I'd have spoken to you sooner." Nate took a deep breath before continuing. "For what it's worth, Rafe, I'm damned glad she's in a safe place. I've been worried about her. She's burning the candle at both ends trying to get ahead financially before she gets laid off."

"Is that inevitable?"

"Yes. It's only a matter of time. Tom Ross, the owner

of the cargo company, is being pressured to reduce his work force in advance of the merger. When I called to check her reference, Tom told me Reagan is the best worker he has. He'd much rather cut others. Unfortunately, the airport has a union, so she'll be the first to go. And that's coming sooner rather than later."

"And let me guess. Her landlord is hoping she'll move so he can rent the space to skiers for an inflated price."

"Probably. His rental business has exploded over the past few years, but his integrity has declined in equal measure." Nate sounded as frustrated as Rafe felt. There wasn't a chance in hell the man was going to fix the heat in her apartment.

After speaking with Nate, Rafe took a quick shower and changed into casual wear. Landon and Savanah's reception wasn't formal, but that didn't mean he felt comfortable wearing his leathers. Moving back to the main part of the house, Rafe smiled to himself when he caught the scent of peaches. Damn, he could get used to her being here. Stepping into the kitchen, he froze at the sight greeting him.

Chapter Three

REAGAN LEANED AGAINST the dark gray marble countertop gazing out the floor to ceiling window. Rafe's home was at the edge of town, so the street light in front did very little to block the spectacular view from the back. The black velvet night was the perfect backdrop for the stars dancing in the sky, their twinkling lights looking like diamonds someone had scattered carelessly over the surface.

"Beautiful." She'd only whispered the words and was shocked when Rafe responded from the other side of the room.

"Stunning."

Spinning around, she watched him walk toward her, his steps measured and purposeful. God in heaven, he was a feast for her hungry eyes. It had been so long since a man looked at her with raw lust. Her boss at the cargo company had always regarded her like a father would a daughter he was proud of…at least until recently. Now she saw regret in his eyes and hated the change.

"I was talking about the sky." Her whispered words faded when he shook his head.

"It pales in comparison, sweetness." The periwinkle halter dress she wore molded to her gentle curves. Her nipples hardened when Rafe used the tip of his finger to trace the edge of the supple fabric hiding her from his view. "This is a very modest dress for a function at a kink club."

He was right. The dress was modest by club standards, but so were the other outfits the Ledek's had given her to wear. She was grateful they'd agreed to ease her into displaying more of her scarred flesh. So far, she hadn't been forced to answer many questions because only a few of the marks were visible, but the questions would come as her clothing became more revealing.

RAFE COULDN'T REMEMBER the last time he'd been rendered speechless by a woman's appearance. As a plastic surgeon, he dealt with beauty on a daily basis. He'd learned early in his medical career how true the saying about beauty being skin deep often was. But something about Reagan Walsh was very special—a unique spark that shined from the depth of her soul.

He'd stood back for several seconds, just looking on as she stared into the night, and wondered what she was thinking. There were few things in the world that could compare with the night sky in Montana, but it had nothing on the vision before him.

The slender woman standing in front of the window would be even more breathtaking with a few added pounds. He'd moved around her small apartment while he'd waited for her to pack and fumed when he'd seen how little food she had in her pantry. Obviously, she was living on as little as possible, trying to save money.

The dress she wore covered more skin than he'd like, and Rafe found himself wondering why she'd been given something this conservative to wear. Thinking back, he realized everything he'd seen her in was similarly modest. It was unlike the Ledeks to allow their help to dress in anything but full-blown fetish wear.

Rafe was thrilled with her response to his touch. Her nipples peaked between one beat of her heart and the next. Her pupils dilated as her pulse pounded at the base of her exposed neck. *Perfect.*

"Are you ready to go? I know you don't have to work for a while yet, but I'd like to extend our date and go in early." Her cheeks turned a sweet shade of pink, and he smiled. Pressing a kiss to her forehead, Rafe whispered, "Your blush speaks volumes, Peach. It makes me want to corrupt you." Her quiet gasp sent a surge of blood to his cock. She drew him in like a magnet to steel, but he'd promised himself to give her time to get to know him. Just because he'd been thinking about her for the past few months didn't mean she'd had the same yearnings.

"Yes, I'd like that, and I'm ready despite being reluctant to leave the warmth of your home."

He pulled her into his arms and kissed the top of her head. "I promise to keep you warm, Peach." Before they stepped back into the garage, he helped her into the light jacket she'd worn and then wrapped her in one of his goose down ski jackets. He chuckled when the coat nearly swallowed her whole. "You look like someone's kid sister."

"I'm too grateful to care about a fashion faux pas."

"Good enough. We'll see about getting you something warmer tomorrow." He felt her still at his words. Cupping her shoulders, Rafe turned her until she was facing him. "Don't, Peach. Don't overthink it. Knowing you are warm and comfortable is important to me. Consider it entirely selfish, because I won't rest easy unless I know you are safe—and having a proper coat during a Montana winter is a safety issue, I assure you."

Their conversation during the short drive to the club was easy, and Rafe found himself enjoying her quick wit. She'd teased him when she learned the extent of his home's technological perks. "Let me guess, you are friends with Phoenix Morgan." When he cast a sideways look at her, she laughed. "I haven't met him, but I've heard a lot about him from club members. It seems there is a diabolical side to his genius."

"Obviously, you've been hearing about some of his more intimate inventions. The upgrades to my home pale in comparison." He hadn't used any of his friend's inventions, but Rafe had spoken with several Doms who swore the next to the youngest Morgan brother had missed his calling. "I've watched a couple of scenes where his internal devices were used. It appeared the submissives' involved were more than satisfied in the end."

Her giggle filled the vehicle, making him smile. "Why do I get the feeling what you *didn't* say has more meaning than what you *did*?"

"Wise woman."

They'd barely made it through the door when Reagan was pulled aside by Savannah Nixon and Kodi Ledek. The two women were in full-on party planning mode, and he reluctantly released Reagan into their care. Turning his attention to the two women, he gave them a stern warning. "Fifteen minutes, ladies. That's all you've got before I want Reagan back at my side. You'll have her undivided attention once again when her shift begins." Their eyes went wide, darting from Reagan and then back to him before nodding.

Rafe watched the three of them scurry past the buffet

tables into the back storeroom. Turning his attention back to the club's main room, he didn't waste any time finding Nate. They stepped into one of the small alcoves at the edge of the larger central area where they could speak privately, but still watch the room from behind the two-way mirror.

"Make it quick. I only gave Kodi and Savannah fifteen minutes to return Reagan to me. I want to spend time with her before she begins working." Rafe wanted to find out as much as he could about Reagan. He didn't want to make any missteps with her.

Nate raised a brow, but didn't comment on Rafe's impatience. "If you are serious about pursuing a relationship with Reagan, there are things you need to know." Rafe didn't respond, because it seemed pointless. *Just spit it out already.* "Reagan was very forthcoming about her background when she was interviewed for the job. I'll let her tell you about her education and career background. But as one of the owners of Mountain Mastery, I feel obligated to inform Doms when they are facing potential challenges with new subs."

"Can the PC BS, Nate, and get to the fucking point." Hell, since when had his friend decided to lace his speech with politically correct bull shit and waltz around a subject like a fucking ballroom dancer?

Letting out a put-upon sigh, Nate looked out the window into the main playroom. "Reagan was attacked a year ago while volunteering in a state prison facility in Texas. Some evidence suggests the attack was set up by the facility's head of security—or, at the very least, he knew in advance and didn't do anything to prevent it. He'd been hitting on her for months, and she'd finally threatened to go public. The inmate who attacked Reagan was somehow allowed access to a secured area inside the infirmary. It was the room where surgical instruments were kept, including the scalpel he used during the attack. She activated her panic alarm, but the Major didn't send in help for almost fifteen minutes."

Rafe couldn't breathe. Just thinking about what she'd had to endure terrified him, and he hadn't even been given the all details yet. "Tell me they hung the fuckers. The attacker and the bastard who let him get to her." His vision was going red with rage on her behalf.

"The attacker was already serving a life sentence, so the additional time was a non-issue. And from what I've heard, the Texas Department of Corrections is still rallying around their staff so it's unlikely anyone will ever be held accountable." Nate ran his hand through his hair in obvious frustration. "Listen, I'm only telling you this because I don't want you to accidently trip over some trigger and be blindsided. Reagan has never taken advantage of the membership that comes with her employment, so we don't know for sure how she'll react during a scene."

"I want a copy of her limit list. I'll review it with her before we play." He paused and turned his attention to the window, watching the three women smiling as they walked back into the large room. "I appreciate the heads-up, Nate. I'm not sure how to explain it, but she is important. I've spent several weeks pulling together some time off in hopes I'd be able to spend more than a couple of evenings getting to know her." Grasping the door knob, Rafe stopped. "Is Kelsey still a member?"

"No. Stalking you gave us all we needed to terminate her membership. Why? Is she giving you trouble again?" The lines between Nate's brows showed his concern. The fiasco with Kelsey had spiraled out of control so fast no one had seen it coming. "She has been back as a guest, but Taz cautioned the Dom about what he was getting himself in to." Nate tilted his head to the side and narrowed his eyes. "Has something happened?"

"She and Reagan are co-workers. I haven't spoken to Reagan about it, yet, but they are apparently friendly enough to share rides to the airport. When Kelsey saw me walking toward the cargo company's office this afternoon, she took off and left Reagan without a ride."

"They've been forecasting this weather change for days. I'd say I'm surprised she left Reagan to walk, but I'm not. Kelsey Jones is one of the most narcissistic women I've ever met. Taz despises her. He insists she's running some sort of scam, but he can't get a bead on it." Nate's younger brother Taz was one of the most gifted empaths Rafe had ever met. His ability to connect with people had been entirely random before Kodi entered their lives. From what Rafe had gathered, both Nate and Taz's skills had improved exponentially since they'd found her. If Taz felt there was something nefarious taking place, it was a safe bet.

"She is deeply disturbed. I'm not sure how she'd be diagnosed, but some of her dots don't seem to be connected, that's for sure."

"Taz wasn't that charitable. He called her bat-shit crazy. And no offense, Doc, but I tend to think his assessment might be more accurate."

Rafe shook his head in amusement at Nate's comment, even though he was certain his friend hadn't been kidding. Rafe didn't think they'd seen Kelsey's worst, and now that he'd made his interest in Reagan public, he hoped he hadn't painted a target on her back.

Chapter Four

DR. TALLY TYSON followed her Master into the large room. Senator Karl Tyson had returned to Montana an hour ago after a month in Washington D.C., and she'd been looking forward to spending some time alone with him. But her loving husband had been uncharacteristically insistent they attend Landon and Savannah's reception. *Figures, all I want to do is bump uglies and he want to socialize.* When she realized how far her thoughts had strayed, Tally let her gaze move around the room and sighed with relief when she didn't see Master Taz anywhere close. *Damn, that mind reading thing is fucking unhandy. I don't know how Kodi puts up with it.*

"I know you are frustrated, but you need to snap out of it. Good things come to those who are obedient." She fought the urge to roll her eyes...barely. "Good save, pet." He tucked her hand in the crook of his arm and headed to the bar. "Come. I have someone I want you to meet. I know you've missed having a third, and I'd like you to meet a man I think might be a good fit for us."

Her feet planted themselves firmly on the cement floor, surprising him. "Really? You've been thinking about that while dealing with all the nonsense going on in D.C.?"

He turned looking down at her and smiled. "Baby, you belong to me. Your happiness is my number one concern.

Always. I'm never too busy to think about what I can do to make your life better, my love."

Tally's eyes filled with tears at the sincerity of his words. She'd never figured out what she'd done to deserve Karl's love. From the moment she'd met him, she'd known he was the other half of her heart and soul. There wasn't anyone in the world who understood her better. At one time, Landon Nixon had been a close second…in many ways. But he'd pulled away from the relationship before Savannah came back into his life. And as much as she missed him, she understood. He deserved the happiness he found with Savannah, and Tally was grateful she and Landon's bride were becoming friends. It had been a bit rocky in the beginning. But they really were a lot alike in many ways.

"Pet, tonight is only a meet and greet. I'm not sure it will work. The man we're talking to isn't sure where he's going to land, although Nate and Taz are working hard to bring him on masochist board their Prairie Winds team. If he does join, his schedule will be unpredictable, but he's said he'd be willing to coordinate his with mine."

Everything he said piqued her interest, and she had to fight back the urge to scan the room. She hadn't realized how much she'd missed the dynamic a third added to their relationship, something both she and Karl enjoyed. Tally recognized a true polyamorous relationship like the Ledeks would never work for them, and she was also certain the special connection they'd experienced with Landon Nixon would be difficult to replicate.

As if he'd read her mind, Karl pushed his fingers through her loose blonde hair until his palm cupped the side of her head, his thumb caressing her cheek. "Don't expect to duplicate what we had with Master Landon, sweetness. Tonight, we need to focus on establishing rapport. Building from that point will be easier."

He was right. She couldn't expect anyone to be exactly like Landon. No two people were exactly alike. She'd met the West twins, and if mirror image twins could be so different, it would be fundamentally unfair to expect strangers to be the same. Nodding her agreement, she looked into his eyes and fell into them, just as she did every time. "Thank you for the reminder. You always know just what I need, and I'm grateful even when I forget to tell you."

His expression softened before he enfolded her into his embrace. "You are the best thing in my life, sweetness. It's getting harder and harder to be apart." He'd made it clear he wasn't comfortable knowing they were going to be separated during his upcoming trip to Columbia, and she was intuitive enough to sense he wanted to know she had a solid support system behind her in case things didn't go well. A shiver of foreboding slithered up her spine, but she pushed it aside not wanting to ruin his first night home.

KOI MEADOWS WATCHED Senator Tyson and his lovely wife enter the room. He'd been introduced to Dr. Tally Tyson at his sister, Kodi's, wedding, but he'd never spoken to her beyond a polite greeting. Yet here he was, waiting to be re-introduced for a much more personal reason.

Tally was petite by any standard, but no one around her seemed to notice. Koi suspected her personality negated the aura of vulnerability he saw at this distance. Her blonde hair cascaded down her back in a flurry of waves and curls, making him wonder what it would be like to thread his fingers through those tempting tresses. Her heart-shaped face and wide eyes made her seem more like a college coed than a well-respected surgeon.

When his younger sister announced her plans to marry Nate and Taz Ledek, Koi hadn't been as shocked as he probably should have. He'd known Kodi had latched on to his stories of the two former SEALs with a level of interest she hadn't shown for any of the other Special Forces members he'd mentioned. And anyone who spent any time at all with the Ledeks could easily recognize the two gifted brothers in her debut novel.

Damn, he was proud of her writing success. He'd known he was a sexual Dominant a long time ago so the content didn't bother him. She'd quizzed him on numerous occasions about points of protocol, and he'd agreed to answer her questions as long as they weren't about his personal practices. *Hopefully, she'll have other sources for that information now, and I'll be off the hook.*

His recent conversations with Karl Tyson had revolved almost entirely around what his expectations were for a third in their relationship. As a U.S. Senator, Koi had expected discretion to be his number one concern, but it hadn't been. Karl had focused on the support he wanted for Tally during his increasingly frequent absences. "She is young and often needs a loving hand to reign in her enthusiasm. She can be rash and frequently shows little regard for her own well-being when I'm away." Koi had easily translated Karl's remarks to "she'll work herself into an early grave without someone watching out for her." He could fucking relate. Koi had done the same thing for more than a decade.

TALLY FOLLOWED HER Master to the bar and felt a rush of heat when she realized who they were meeting. She'd been introduced to Kodi's brother at her wedding, but they'd never gotten past polite greetings. Scrambling to pull information from her memory, Tally recalled Koi Meadows had been a Navy SEAL before switching to the CIA. When she'd asked Kodi how she felt about the change, her friend had sighed as tears filled her dark eyes. "While he was a SEAL, I never knew where he was or when he'd be back. But at least I took some comfort in the fact he was fighting as part of a group of soldiers. Once he switched to the Agency, I reasoned his enemies might fewer, but they'd be sneakier. Never let it be said I can't rationalize with the best of them."

While Tally saw numerous holes in Kodi's reasoning, she hadn't pointed them out. It was clearly a coping mechanism for her sweet friend, and who was Tally to burst her bubble? By the time they stopped in front of Koi, he was already standing. His dark gaze focused so fiercely on her she could have sworn she felt the heat, and he hadn't even touched her.

"What was going through your mind between here and the door, *ma poupée*?" *My little doll?* Well, there were certainly worse things he could call her. But what the hell happened to *hello*? "Tally? Even though this is a casual meeting, we're still in a BDSM club. Answer my question." The command in his voice wasn't sharp, nor had it been accompanied by anything other than a steely determination to get the answer.

"I was thinking about a conversation I had with your sister. I'd asked her if she worried more when you were a SEAL or after you went to work for the Agency. Her explanation surprised me." She could tell by his startled expression that she'd surprised him. *Good. You want to forego social niceties, like a greeting, you deserve to be surprised by blatant honesty.*

The seconds ticked by as he studied her, and she returned his stare. *Meet and greet, my ass. This is going to turn into a power struggle of the first order if I don't contain it.* When she finally dropped her gaze, Tally heard Karl's soft chuckle. "Pet, I believe your worries might have been premature. It seems Master Koi and Master Landon may be more alike than I assumed." The man standing in front of her might not hear the relief in her husband's voice, but it was there.

Tally kept her eyes downcast until Koi used his fingers to lift her chin. "Look at me, *ma poupée*." His dark eyes were softer now than they'd been seconds ago. And Tally could see the same tenderness in them she often saw in Kodi's when she watched Nate and Taz. "When you left the other side of the room, your expression was filled with anticipation. But it was obvious the instant you realized who you were meeting because your eyes clouded and you looked like you'd fallen into a sad memory. That's not an emotion I want to see in your eyes, Tally. If things work out as I hope they will, my role will be to enrich your life, not weigh it down."

She felt herself relax and was grateful he'd taken time to explain his concern. Pulling in a deep breath, Tally took a few seconds to put her thoughts in order before giving him a tentative smile. Exhaling, she shifted her focus to Karl. "I hope we can begin again. I feel like I've ruined the evening you'd planned."

"How did you ruin it, pet? By searching that brilliant mind of yours for information about the man you'd been told you were going to meet?" His cajoling tone made her smile.

"Hey, big brother. Tally looked a little shell-shocked a minute ago. What did you do?" Kodi stepped up next to her brother and pulled him down to press a kiss against his tan cheek.

"Ayasha, don't stir up trouble." Nate's deep voice sounded over Tally's shoulder, making her jump. "Sorry, sweetness, but my lovely wife will take full advantage of the fact we're hosting a vanilla party if I don't watch her. And poking her brother is one of her favorite pastimes. We'll never convince him to join our team if she doesn't lighten up."

Glancing back at the woman many considered her co-conspirator, Tally giggled at the faux look of innocence on her face. Koi watched his sister, affection shining bright in his dark eyes. "Kodi, that look hasn't worked on me since you used it to get out of the first day of kindergarten. Damn, Mom and Dad were mad I took you to school with me instead of leaving you off at the grade school."

"They shouldn't have grounded you. You were being a sweet big brother."

"I was being a gullible big brother. Being stuck at home for two weeks gave me plenty of time to watch you work your magic on Mom and Dad, *mon coeur*."

Kodi melted against her brother and whispered, "You're my heart, too, brother mine. You'll always be the first man I loved." Tally watched the interaction with a mixture of awe and envy. What she wouldn't have given to have a brother who adored her like Koi did Kodi.

"Whatever. As long as my brother and I are the last men you love, it's all good." Nate pulled Kodi back to his side and shook Koi's hand. "Welcome back, Koi. Enjoy the party. We'll talk in the morning."

After the Ledeks walked away, Koi returned his attention to her. "I like this expression much better, *ma poupée*. Let's get something to drink and find a quiet place to talk." Tally felt Karl's hand press against her lower back, the tips of his fingers grazing the crack of her ass and reminding her how little she was wearing. The dress was conservative as far as club wear was concerned, but it would be scandalous at the D.C. parties that were such an integral part of her husband's world. Tally was fully aware the time was rapidly approaching when she was going to be asked to move back to the east coast, but she intended to stall as long as possible.

Pushing those thoughts aside, she picked up her margarita and let Karl and Koi lead her to one of the more secluded seating arrangements. She suddenly realized how much she was looking forward to seeing where this evening led.

Chapter Five

REAGAN FELT HIS piercing gaze before she saw him across the room. Rafe Newell's focus on her was even more intense inside the club than during dinner. Kodi Ledek nudged her and whispered, "Damn, girl. Master Rafe lasered in on you the minute we stepped through the door. Holy hell fire, that's one hot man."

Savannah laughed from Reagan's other side. "I hear a book bubbling to the surface. Don't tell her anything you don't want distributed to the masses, Reagan."

"Hey! I'm not that bad...usually."

"Always." Reagan found herself laughing at the two friends as they squabbled good naturedly between themselves. She hadn't had any close friends since graduating from college and was surprised how much she'd missed the easy camaraderie that came from shared experiences.

"We had dinner together, and he's letting me sleep in his..." Reagan stopped abruptly when she realized the other two women were no longer walking beside her. Turning, she found them staring at her as if she'd just sprouted another head. "What?"

Savannah leaned close to Kodi, but didn't bother to lower her voice. "Is she really that clueless?"

"I'm wondering if she isn't a plant. Maybe an actress studying for a role and my husbands didn't tell me."

"Maybe, but why didn't she start here right away instead of wasting all that time at the airport?"

"Good point. No clue."

Savannah sighed. "She seems bright, but I've been fooled before."

Reagan had finally heard enough and burst out laughing at the two wannabe comedians standing in front of her. "What? He just didn't want me to stay in my apartment because the furnace isn't working."

Kodi rolled her eyes. "Yeah. Like we don't have any spare bedrooms."

Savannah giggled before adding, "A couple of them might even be upstairs in your suite."

"Wench. You aren't supposed be thinking about anything but your Master."

"You are exactly right, Kodi." One of Landon Nixon's arms encircled his new bride as his other hand turned her chin so he could kiss her. When he finally released her, Savannah's entire body almost shimmered...as if electrified. Reagan couldn't turn away from the intimacy. *That. That's exactly what I want. Someone who looks at me the way he does her.*

Reagan felt Rafe's warmth before he spoke. How had she known it was him? Her mind hadn't worked it through before his voice floated over her shoulder. "Are you all right, Peach? You seemed a million miles away just now." Without thinking, she turned toward him and sucked in a breath when his lips brushed her own. *Leaping leprechauns, how did he get so close without me realizing he was here?*

She'd have been embarrassed if she hadn't seen the flare of desire darken his eyes. Pulling in a calming breath, she nodded. "Yes, Sir. I'm fine. I was just watching the newlyweds..." She didn't finish the thought. Anything she could have said would have sounded sappy.

"Finish it, Peach. No hiding." When she dropped her gaze, a low rumble that sounded a lot like a growl reverberated from his chest. Using his fingers under her chin, Rafe brought her face back up until she was forced to meet his gaze. "Talk to me, Reagan. Be brave. Take a chance."

How long had it been since she'd trusted someone enough to be completely transparent? At one time, she'd been an open book, but her experience in Texas had changed her in too many ways to count. The attack had been a huge factor, but the fallout afterward had been more devastating than any of the physical injuries. He didn't ask again, but he didn't let her turn away, either.

"I was thinking how wonderful it must be to share such a close connection." She closed her eyes when his hands framed her face, his thumbs brushing over her cheeks. The soothing touch helped steady her, and despite the fact they were surrounded by other people, everyone else had faded to the background.

"Thank you, Peach. Your honesty is gift, and I know that was hard for you to admit. But let me assure you, I envy their connection as well. The depth and intensity of D/s relationships is one of my favorite aspects of the lifestyle." He gave her a few minutes to just breathe, but when she gave him a small smile, he nodded as if he understood she was ready to move on.

"Come on. I want to enjoy the party before you start working." She was relieved to step back from the heat of the moment. It wasn't wise to fall for a man she'd basically just met. Not to mention the fact he hadn't seen her scars yet. She'd only gone to lunch with one man since she'd moved to Montana, and it turned out he'd wanted to sell her life insurance. Oh yes, indeed, that was a big boost for a girl's ego.

Walking among the club's members as a guest was a strange feeling. Reagan lost herself for a moment while Rafe spoke to a small group of Dungeon Monitors. They were discussing club business, but she'd zoned out when they closed ranks and started speaking quietly among themselves. When she absently reached for a couple of empty glasses set on a small table, Rafe's hand closed over her wrist. "No, Reagan. You aren't working, baby. I'm sorry I left you alone so long. Obviously, my social skills are a bit rusty. Come."

RAFE COULDN'T BELIEVE he'd gotten so lost in conversation with the Dungeon Monitors he'd abandoned Reagan. When he'd seen her unconsciously reach for the glasses, he'd moved to intercept. Damn, he felt like a first-class prick. It had taken him weeks to get up the courage to ask her to dinner, and then he left her to her own devices until she resorted to clean-up duty. He could only imagine what his mother or sister would say—and none of the words running through his head were anything pleasant.

Leading her to the side of the room, Rafe kept her wrist shackled in his hand and was encouraged by the small tremor he felt move through her. After talking with Nate, he'd wondered if she'd ever consent to any form of bondage, but her reaction gave him hope. Rafe wasn't a rope master, but he couldn't imagine having a submissive who rejected all forms of bondage. Securing a sub to a St. Andrew's cross or spanking bench was not only part of his kink, it was also for their safety. Too much movement could cause the Dominant to misjudge the distance, landing a blow much harder than he or she had intended.

When he reached one of the few shadowed alcoves around the room that would afford them a small semblance of privacy, he pulled her in front of him. With her back to the room, she'd be forced to focus on him. "I'm sorry." She blinked at him in surprise before her eyes went glassy with unshed tears.

"Don't be. I should have stayed closer and not been daydreaming. But when you all closed ranks in that little circle, I felt like I was eavesdropping." She took a shuddering breath before continuing. "I haven't been to many social functions since…well, for a long time. And the only time I've been to the club, aside from working, was when I was first interviewed for the job."

"And then I insisted we come early so we can spend some time together, extending our date, and promptly leave you alone. Great first date impression I'm making." His last words were barely audible, but the softening of the lines around her mouth told him she'd heard his self-disparaging remark. "I have a thousand questions I'd like to ask you, but I'm going to pick and choose in the interest of time."

For a second, he thought she was going to back away from him. There'd been a flash of hesitance bordering on fear in her eyes that nearly made him revise his plan. But the old adage advising "begin as you intend to go" moved through his mind, and Rafe decided to stay the course.

"First, I want you to tell me one thing about what happened in Texas." When she gasped, he wrapped his hand around the base of her skull. "I'm not asking for the full story now. I just want you to share one thing that comes to mind. In my line of work, I often deal with survivors of trauma, and I've learned each piece of information they share makes it easier to let go of the next bit. And I want to start that process with you. You are worth it, baby."

Her eyes were glassy again, but her whispered thanks spoke volumes. "I figured Master Nate would tell you. I suppose he had to. I read about triggers in an erotic romance novel. Not much I can do about that, I guess. Damn, I was hoping to avoid this…at least for a while. Suck it up and spit it out, Reagan."

Rafe smiled at her revealing self-talk. "Just one thing, Peach."

"The worst part was the betrayal by the staff who was supposed to protect me."

Rafe struggled to hide his surprise. He'd expected any number of responses—fear for her life, pain, or nightmares, just to name a few. But the fact she'd first thought of the betrayal by those charged with her safety was as shocking as it was enlightening.

Pulling her close, Rafe wrapped his arms around her in a reassuring hug. "You amaze me, Peach. Your answer makes perfect sense, but I must admit it wasn't what I expected. I'm honored that you trusted me enough to answer so honestly." Honored was a monumental understatement. "Your response tells me a lot about you, and I'm damned impressed with what I heard."

He released her and put just enough space between them so he could look into her eyes. "Last question, then we'll dance. Tell me there isn't another man in your life I'm going to have to push aside."

Reagan smiled and shook her head. "No. I wouldn't have agreed to go to dinner with you if I was seeing someone else. I'm sure you can tell from my answer to your first question…loyalty is a huge issue for me."

He leaned his head forward until their foreheads were touching. "Perfect. I'm happy to know I don't have to start looking for places to hide a body. Messy."

"Very. And difficult to explain to your friends when you call them in the middle of the night asking for plastic bags, duct tape, and shovels."

Rafe laughed out loud and turned to walk the short distance to the dance floor. He rarely danced at the club, because the music they usually played didn't lend itself well to the type of dancing he preferred. His grandmother's voice drifted through his mind. *"It's not dancing if you aren't holding a woman in your arms, Rafe. Kids now days don't know anything about romance."* Vowing to honor her memory, Rafe pulled Reagan into his arms and led her around the large dance floor in a slow waltz. He sent up silent thanks for his grandmother's insistence he learn ballroom dancing. It hadn't felt like a gift at the time, but he was reaping the benefits now.

"Are you interested in learning more about Dominance and submission, Reagan?" He'd leaned close so his words brushed over the shell of her ear. Her shudder was an answer, but he waited patiently for her to verbally respond—and didn't have to wait long.

"Yes, Sir." Her answer made his cock tighten in need, and he was sure she felt it jerk against her stomach.

"I'd like to introduce you to the lifestyle, Peach. We'll discuss it further after you get off work. For now, I want to hold you close. I've wanted you in my arms for a long time." Her quick inhalation let him know he'd surprised her. *Good. People surprise me all the damned time.*

Chapter Six

REAGAN LEANED AGAINST the wall in the storage room and sighed. She'd worked all day at the cargo company, eaten dinner with Rafe, discovered her apartment was only fit for a friggin' penguin, and danced for almost two hours. Then she'd switched gears and started working the second shift of the Nixons' party. Things were winding down, but she'd needed a minute to catch her breath before the next wave of toasts was completed. The more this crew drank, the more relaxed they were becoming with protocol, which had already been toned down because it was a celebration rather than a play party.

"Hey, Reagan. Can you get that box of flutes off the top shelf?" Dixie was one of the club's regular servers, and she'd also worked a full day before pulling a double shift for the party. Reagan had heard the woman was putting herself through school and agreed to take all the extra shifts she could during her brief breaks between semesters.

Reagan pushed off from the wall and made her way to the shelves as Dixie struggled to uncork a bottle of champagne. "What the heck? The others weren't this hard to open." Reagan had just opened her mouth to ask if the bottle was chilled properly when she heard an ominous crack. Dixie screamed just as the world around Reagan exploded…literally.

Time seemed to slow around her, but Reagan's mind raced at the speed of light. She sent up a silent prayer of thanks Dixie had been using a tall cabinet as a resting place for the bottle. *That should help minimize her injuries. Damn, girl, I hope you covered your face.* Just as those thoughts sped in her mind, a flash of blinding pain seared the backs of her legs and bare back. The step stool she'd been standing on slid out from under her, and Reagan crumbled to the concrete floor, bouncing off everything on the way down.

With her vision dimming, Reagan tried to get her feet under her, but her legs weren't cooperating. She heard the door slam open and the thunder of footsteps as pandemonium broke out on the other side of the cabinet. Breathing a huge sigh of relief, she was grateful they'd found Dixie. Her next thought was a moment of panic. What if they didn't realize she was in here? If Dixie couldn't tell them, she could be stuck here until she gained enough strength to stand. It was too frightening to think about…so Reagan let herself slide into the dim oblivion closing in from all sides.

The next time she tried to move, a low groan vibrated through her chest and warm hands held her still. "Don't move, baby. I'm not finished assessing your injuries."

"Rafe?"

"Yes, Peach, now be a good girl and stay still for me."

How long was I out? They're going to ask, and I don't know.

"Reagan, I know exactly how long you were out. I was already beside you when you closed those beautiful brown eyes, baby." His fingers were running over every inch of her face, frown lines forming between his brows. "We'll get the pictures, but I don't think you have any serious breaks. You are going to look like hell for a while. Do you remember what happened, Reagan?"

"Champagne grenade."

Her eyes were drifting closed again, so she didn't see his reaction, but she felt him stiffen against her. His hands were still moving over her. "We're going to chat about your terminology, Peach. I obviously have a lot to learn about you." Rafe's quietly spoken words faded into the background when she realized they were no longer alone.

Reagan surfaced momentarily as she was being rolled from the club, and she panicked. Dark memories crashed over her in a tidal wave of fear. She'd done this once before. Being taken away by first responders she didn't know to a hospital she'd never been in, surrounded by strangers…it was all too familiar and frightening.

"Rafe?"

Her startled cry brought a squeeze to her hand. "Right here, baby. I'm going with you to the hospital. I have staff privileges there." *What? He's a doctor? Wait. I knew this. I remember. He's a doctor in San Francisco.* "I'm not sure you meant to say all of that out loud, Peach." His soft chuckle warmed her from the inside out. *Nope, sure don't mean to blab every little thought that traipses through my head. Damn!*

"I don't ordinarily tell people at the club what I do for a living, Reagan. Though I'm not surprised you know considering airports are usually rife with gossip. I don't tell my patients about my lifestyle choices, either. But keeping my life so compartmentalized has become increasingly difficult. That's one of the reasons I'm considering relocating my practice to Montana."

Reagan hoped the small smile that floated through her pain soaked mind made its way to the surface, because she didn't have the energy to make it happen otherwise.

Rafe wasn't worried about the abrasions on Reagan's face—they'd heal soon enough. And the bruises were already turning shades of deep blue. She'd be uncomfortable and damned colorful for a while, but there wouldn't be any lasting effects. The lacerations on her back and legs were another matter.

He'd directed the ambulance to transport Reagan to the hospital farther north because that was where Ryan Morgan practiced. Rafe had toured the facility a few months ago and been pleasantly surprised by the updates. From what he'd learned, it was on the way to living up to its Regional Hospital moniker.

Before the paramedics had even gotten Reagan unloaded, Ryan stepped up beside him. "What the hell happened? Nate said it sounded like C4."

"Fucking champagne. I can't tell you how many of these I see." God knew the social set he catered to loved their bubbly and had rarely been advised how important it was to keep it ice cold so it could be uncorked safely. The industry had made some changes that helped, but education was the key.

"We'll triage and then send her to surgery. I've already called in a team for you." Rafe nodded his thanks. Ryan Morgan was damned good at his job. It was almost a shame he was slowly being shifted to the administrative side and away from direct patient care.

"I'll help assess then scrub. She's going to be in surgery a long time so I want to make sure I know everything there is to know. The lacerations are deep, and most aren't straight." It was going to take longer to close the wounds because he planned to layer the sutures and then seal the tops to minimize scarring. She already had significant scarring in some of the affected areas, and that was going to further complicate his work.

During the next half hour, the small hospital's dedicated staff moved at a clipped pace. Their motions were almost military in their precision, and Rafe smiled when he realized why. Ryan Morgan had been in medical school when he'd enlisted in the Navy as a result of the 9/11 terrorist attacks. Nate and Taz praised his medic skills, stating many of their SEAL team members owed their lives to his ability to improvise under the worst possible conditions. He'd eventually resigned his commission and returned to finish medical school before moving to Montana.

Rafe took a moment to step back and watch things with an assessing eye and found himself impressed with what he saw. Sure, the facility was small, but the equipment was up to date and well-maintained. "We just got her blood work back. Since I'm not sure how much she lost or how much you may need during surgery, I've called in a donor."

"Called in a donor? What the hell? You have a calling tree for donations?" Rafe knew he'd been had when he turned to see the glint of mischief in Ryan's eyes.

"Yep, we're all big-city slick here. I have a chart on the back of my office door. Made it myself with a new box of crayons, construction paper, and a glue stick."

"Christ, you're a wise ass just like all the other Morgans. I feel sorry for your mother and aunt. Genetics can be a real bitch." Rafe chuckled at the satisfied smile on Ryan's face. The other man had been trying to lighten the mood, and Rafe appreciated the effort.

"She is a perfect match for Brandt. He's already down in the lab. Joelle will pamper him tonight, and he'll soak it all up like a fucking sponge—the jerk." Rafe shook his head. It amazed him how easily his friends seemed to maneuver through the intricacies of polyamorous relationships.

Rafe stepped back up to the table and brushed his fingers over Reagan's cheek. "I'm going to go shower and scrub for surgery, baby. The next time we talk, you'll be all patched up."

Her eyelids fluttered open, but he didn't think she was focused enough to actually see him against the lights. Reaching up, he switched off the one shining too close, and she whispered her thanks. "You're going to assist? That's sweet."

"No, Peach. I'm your surgeon. We'll talk more later." Her eyes widened in surprise, but it quickly dimmed as she let herself slip back into sleep. He didn't think her concussion was an issue, but they'd been waking her every few minutes just to be sure, and he wanted her to get all the rest she could. The next few days weren't going to be much fun for her, and rest would go a long way to setting her on the road to recovery.

He pressed a lingering kiss to her smooth forehead and turned back to Ryan. "Let's go."

Walking side by side down the hall, Ryan slanted him a sideways glance. "Ever operated on someone you cared about before?"

"No, why?"

"It's a whole new ballgame, I assure you." Rafe didn't respond. Not because he disagreed, but because he didn't...not necessarily. But he didn't agree, either.

"You'll see. But consider yourself warned, and you'll buy the beer when this is done and you're forced to admit I was right."

"What are you going to be right about this time, Master?" The soft female voice behind them had Ryan turning on his heel.

"Oh, baby, look at you." He pulled her into his arms and kissed her with enough heat Rafe was tempted to move away. "You've come to pick up Brandt? Damn, he is going to milk this for all its worth. Lucky fucker."

Her soft laugh filled the narrow hallway. "I promise to make it up to you." Joelle turned her attention to Rafe and smiled. "I'm so glad you're here. I don't know Reagan very well, but from what I've heard, she is a sweetheart."

"She is and thanks for your vote of confidence. I'd love to visit, but I need to get ready."

She nodded and then said, "We live nearby and have plenty of room. After she's settled and you're satisfied she won't evaporate into a fine mist without you, we'll talk about finding you a real bed so you can rest."

Joelle Morgan was every bit as brilliant as her Nobel Prize implied. She'd known he'd stick to Reagan like glue for the first twenty-four hours. After that, the post-surgery team would be able to handle the next shift. He'd need to get some real sleep. Since he planned to take her home with him, there wouldn't be any concerns about her post-facility care.

"Thank you, Joelle. I'll take you up on that offer as soon as I'm comfortable leaving. She's going to be in surgery quite a while, so I won't leave the hospital for the first twenty-four hours. But after that, I'll be headed your way." Her face brightened in a smile as if she hadn't expected him to accept her offer, but was pleased he had.

Before he could turn away, Joelle laid her slender fingers on his arm, warming his skin through the dress shirt he was wearing. "I hope it works out for you, Sir. You deserve someone special." When he raised his brow at her in question, she flashed a brilliant smile. "I've worked with physicians my entire adult life, Dr. Newell. There is a difference in their eyes when they are caring for someone who's close to their heart...a certain softness in their approach. I see a gentle consideration for Reagan. But there is something more. You're also making sure you take care of yourself so you can better care for her. She's lucky to find that...not many of us do."

With that, she turned back to her husband and Master, kissing him quickly before unwrapping herself from his arms. Rafe nodded at Ryan and took his cue to leave. He wanted to review the surgical unit's inventory before he scrubbed to be sure the staff set out his preferred sutures.

Rafe's reputation as one of the leading plastic surgeons in the country was hard earned. He didn't leave details to chance with any patient. And Joelle had been right when she'd noted Reagan was important to him. He wasn't sure where it would lead, but he was determined to find out. Hell, she was the only woman who'd caught his eye in longer than he could remember. Sure, he played at the club, but he rarely fucked the subs he topped.

Striding down the hall, Rafe tried to remember the last woman he'd taken to dinner who wasn't a business contact. Even harder to remember was the last time he'd met a woman as intriguing as Reagan. Shoving all the personal thoughts aside, Rafe pushed through the doors of the hospital's surgical unit and began mentally ticking off everything he'd need.

"Dr. Newell?" Turning to his left, Rafe met soft gray

eyes framed by curly black and silver hair that shone under the brilliant lights. When he nodded, the woman smiled. "I'm Ann Ratcher." She didn't miss his reaction, and she rolled her eyes. "Don't say it. I've been listening to it my entire professional life. Honest to Pete, I should have gotten married just to change my name."

He chuckled and nodded his understanding. "This your unit, Nurse Ann?" Rafe wasn't sure what put the smile on her face—the fact he'd referred to the surgery area as hers or that he'd just assured her that he didn't intend to tease her by calling her Nurse Ratched. He'd had years of experience judging age, and he guessed she was coming up on fifty faster than she wanted to admit.

"Yes, Sir. Doc Ryan might think it's his, but I remember taking care of him when he'd visit his aunt and uncle."

"Surely you aren't suggesting your seniority points stem from age?" He tried his best to appear aghast, but the grin tugging at the corners of his mouth no doubt ruined the look.

Fanning herself in an overly dramatic imitation of an antebellum lady, she intoned a perfect Scarlet O'Hara voice. "Good heavens, no. Fiddle-dee-dee."

Rafe found himself laughing out loud for the first time in hours. As some of the tension drained from him, he noticed she was smiling. "Thanks, Ann. I didn't realize how much I needed that. You're damned perceptive. I hope you'll be assisting."

"I will. I also wanted to make sure we have everything set up the way you prefer. I hope the rumor I heard about you considering relocating your clinic to Montana are true, Dr. Newell, and I'm not above sucking up to help you make the decision."

Rafe grinned. He liked Nurse Ann. Her honesty was

refreshing, but he was keenly aware that she kept her staff on a short leash. Nothing happened in the hospital's O.R. unless it had her personal stamp of approval.

"Duly noted. Let's get started. I use some of the more common sutures sizes, but I'll also be using some very specific things as well. I'm anticipating we'll be here several hours so I want to make sure you staff has eaten before we begin. Restroom breaks need to be kept to a minimum, but if they are rotated, you won't hear any complaints from me."

"I've pulled in a great team, Dr. Newell. I think you'll be pleased." He didn't doubt her. There was a quiet confidence in her tone that he appreciated. She obviously respected the people she worked with, and he'd seen firsthand what an impact that had on morale. Rafe was convinced she'd be his biggest ally and a tremendous asset if he moved.

"Ann, when you are and I are working alone or in social situations, I'd prefer you call me Rafe. I'll let you choose between Dr. Newell and Dr. Rafe when we're in working with other staff or dealing with patients. I'm more interested in building trust between us than I am protocol."

Her expression softened as her eyes registered something deeper than what he'd just said. "We're going to get along wonderfully, Rafe. It's been a long time since I thought about protocol."

Chapter Seven

EXHAUSTION THREATENED TO pull Rafe under, but he pushed away from the wall and stepped up to the bed to smooth the strands of Reagan's hair that managed to escape her braid. Ann had tamed her long hair before securing it under the surgical cap almost twelve hours earlier. It had been an act of compassion, and strange as it sounded, that small gesture had gone further to convince him Montana was the place to move than anything he'd been promised.

"You're dead on your feet, man. Get some rest. I'll sit with her." Rafe turned to find Taz Ledek filling the door frame. It was a testament to how tired he was that he hadn't realized the other man was so close, because he was a fucking giant. "You won't be in any shape to make good judgements if you let my clumsy ass sneak up on you." Rafe chuckled. If there was one thing Taz Ledek wasn't, it was clumsy. Hell, he had more martial arts training than anyone Rafe had ever met. And, as a former Navy SEAL, he was as stealthy as a jungle cat. There was a reason their new wife referred to the brothers as Ninjas.

"Thanks. I think I'll take you up on that offer. She's settled in the past hour." It had taken forever for the post-op pain management to kick in—no doubt she'd been given so much after the attack her tolerance was sky-high.

"I asked the staff to set up a room for me next door." Taz frowned, but didn't respond. "Call me immediately if you need anything. The staff has been great, but I can be an intimidating bastard."

Taz lifted his brow, and Rafe realized how absurd he'd sounded. There were very few people around more intimidating than the six-and-a-half-foot Native American brick wall standing in front of him. "Goddess, man. You're hard on my ego. A pansy-assed city boy and you think you're more intimidating that I am. That's just plain insulting. I'm going to have to start scaring small children and kicking puppies to beef up my rep."

Rafe shook his head and grinned. "I'm going to tell Kodi you said that. That woman has your number, my friend."

"Don't I know it. She owns me. Now, get the hell out of here before I hug you or something. Damned woman is making me soft."

Rafe turned back to Reagan and brushed his fingers over her cheek. She needed to stay sleeping on her stomach, and he doubted the position was natural for her when she continued trying to roll despite the obvious discomfort. "She isn't comfortable on her stomach, but she needs to stay put. If that becomes an issue, the staff can secure her."

"Yeah, because I've never tied a woman to a bed. Fuck me. Get out of here before you tell me how to breathe."

Fatigue was sweeping through him, and Rafe was self-aware enough to realize he wasn't helping at this point. He gave Reagan one last glance, flipped Nate off, and walked out of the room.

"He's gone, doll. You can stop playing opossum now." Taz had known the moment he stepped into the room Reagan was awake. As an empath, he'd felt her rioting emotions before he'd entered. Pain was battering her like a ship in high seas, but she'd somehow managed to maintain the illusion of sleep. "I'll give him five to get out of the hall, and then I'm calling for the nurse. Don't fight it, Reagan. You of all people should understand how important it is for your body to heal unencumbered by pain."

"I know you're right, but I was sure he wouldn't leave unless he thought I was resting comfortably." Her voice was thready, but he heard the sincerity in her tone. Taz shook his head. *Goddess save me from well-meaning submissives.*

"I can assure you, Master Rafe is much more concerned with your health than an extra half-hour rest. As your friend and employer, I want you comfortable so you'll recover as quickly as possible. But as Rafe's friend, I appreciate your concern for him as well. I'll make you a deal. I won't throw your sweet ass under the bus if you promise to ask for the help in the future when you need it."

When she'd agreed, he reached forward and pressed the call button. Once they'd sent the nurse for the medication, he pulled a chair close and sat down, putting himself in her line of vision. Anxiety was coming off the little sub in waves, and he didn't think she would rest properly until he got to the bottom of the problem. He'd seen soldiers fight the strongest narcotic painkillers until they were able to set aside whatever was occupying their thoughts.

"What's on your mind, Reagan?" Her eyes filled with tears, and Taz felt like he'd been hit in the chest with a blast of sorrow and fear. *Holy shit.*

"I'm going to lose my job. I've been trying to do everything I could to hold on, but this will be the excuse they need to cut me. I don't have enough money saved up to make it through the winter. And that was before all these medical expenses." Fuck it all, she was breaking his heart. "And I'm whining. I hate it when people whine. It doesn't ever help anything…not ever, really. And I'm still doing it."

"Stop. Take a deep breath, doll." Taz was certain she'd respond to the command in his voice and was pleased to see her eyes widen and her mouth snap shut. "Good girl. One of the interesting things about pain killers is they often act as truth serum. Even if they aren't managing the pain, they can drop all the shields we keep in place. The little bit you've been given is scattering your thinking, even if it isn't keeping you comfortable."

Reagan's eyes were clouded with confusion, and he could feel waves of fear pulsing from her. "I want you to talk to me without falling over the emotional edge you were teetering on—not because I can't handle it, but because I know you'll regret it later. You're a valued employee, Reagan; more importantly, you're my friend, and I don't want that between us once you've recovered. Do you understand?"

Tears slid from the corners of her eyes, soaking the sheet beneath her face. "Don't cry, doll. Kodi will skin me alive if she finds out I caused your tears."

"I'm just overwhelmed. I don't know what I'm going to do. Going back to Texas isn't an option." Taz nodded in silent agreement. Unbelievably, the damned Major at the prison where Reagan had been a volunteer still held his position. From what Taz had heard, the man was also making discreet inquiries trying to find out where she'd moved. He made a mental note to ask Phoenix Morgan to give the fucker something else to think about. Maybe if he was busy trying to repair his crumbling credit rating or returning thousands of dollars in sex toys, he might not have time to think about the woman he'd almost gotten killed.

"Right now, you have one job, and that's to heal. If you lose your position at the cargo company, that means the Universe wants you to go in a different direction. Nate and I had already been tossing around a couple of ideas related to the expansion, and we'd planned to talk to you about them next month." He gave a shrug he hoped would appear nonchalant, but her skeptical expression said he hadn't been successful.

"Don't create a job for me out of sympathy, Taz. That would just make me feel worse." He raised his brow at her in surprise. She'd never called him Taz, always using Sir or Master Taz when she was working. He appreciated the shift and told her so.

Before they could continue their conversation, the nurse was back and, with a quick press of the plunger, sent Reagan into a blissful slumber. "She'll rest now. Dr. Morgan expected her tolerance level to be high. Thank you for alerting us. I hate it when our patients think toughing it out is the way to go." He grinned at the woman who obviously had a big heart.

Settling back in his chair, Taz pulled his phone from his chest pocket and fired off a quick text to his brother. *I'm sitting with Reagan while Rafe gets some rest. He was dead on his feet & only left because I insisted. She belongs to him, even if she doesn't know it yet.*

Nate's response was immediate. *Does Rafe know?*

Yeah, I think so. Hard to tell when he was about to fall asleep standing up.

You tell her about her job at the cargo company? The owner had called them asking if they could put her on full-time. It sounded like he regretted having to let her go, but when Nate reminded him the road to hell was paved with good intentions, the man had disconnected the call. Thank Goddess he couldn't cancel her insurance until the paperwork was done.

No, but she knows it's coming. I've mentioned we want to talk to her.

But she thinks it's charity.

Something like that. Did you get Kodi to make an appointment? They'd been trying to knock up their beautiful bride since the moment she'd agreed to marry them. But so far, each time they'd thought they'd succeeded, they'd been wrong. They were encouraging her to see a specialist, but so far, she'd managed to keep herself *too busy*. Since he could hear her thoughts, Taz understood her fear, but the ostrich approach wasn't going to get her the baby they all wanted desperately.

Yes, but she is spitting mad and standing to finish the final edits on her new book. And before you crawl up my ass— charming her wasn't working. She needed to be pushed, and I obliged.

You're an ass.

Not news. You can be the hero when you get home.

Count on it.

KELSEY GLARED AT her boss's retreating back. After informing her Reagan wouldn't be returning, the old coot had the audacity to say he expected Kelsey to add her former co-worker's duties to her own. Was he insane? Kelsey had shifted her own work to Reagan over the past several months and enjoyed having extra time to spend on her own little sideline venture. But now he expected her to pick up the entire workload? Access to the airport and cargo flights was critical to her enterprise, so she needed this job. But she needed to be able to slip the packages on the flights, and that wasn't always easy.

Perhaps it was time for a little financial insurance. Scrolling through her contacts, she found the name she was looking for. A couple of drinks and Reagan had spilled the beans about the reason she'd left Texas. It hadn't taken Kelsey long to uncover the details, and she'd saved the man's contact information for just such an occasion. *Let's see how badly he wants to know where his obsession landed.*

Chapter Eight

"Two days. I've been stuck in this place for two days. If he doesn't let me out today, I'm going to go postal. Have you ever had to take a shower on just half your body? It's impossible. And I want to wash my damned hair…it's disgusting." Kodi, Savannah, and Tally all grinned from their respective positions around her bed.

Thank God Reagan had finally convinced Rafe to let her turn over, because she'd gotten damned tired of talking to people she couldn't see. "He's hovering over me like he thinks I'm going to escape."

"But isn't that exactly what you're planning to do?" Tally gave her a knowing grin. "I've seen that look in patients' eyes before, Reagan. And you can bet your sweet, soon-to-be-flaming ass, Rafe has, too. He knows if he tells you when he plans to discharge you, you'll jump ship six to twelve hours before. So, he won't tell you." She gave a negligent shrug, and Reagan wanted to slap her silly for being right.

"I got a glimpse of the cuts when I stepped out of the shower before the Nurse Follow-every-order-to-a-tee hustled me out of the bathroom. Evidently, I'm not supposed to see Dr. Newell's fancy repair work until he gives the okay. There aren't any stitches. All I saw was faint red lines. How is that possible?" What she'd seen didn't make any sense to her. It looked like someone had drawn on her back with a red fine-line marker. "I'm still having trouble wrapping my head around the fact one of the most sought-after plastic surgeons in the country is taking care of me."

"I'll bet he'd take care of you in a lot of other ways, too, if you'd let him. And I've heard amazing things about his work. I'll bet you have little or no scaring. There's a reason people fly from all over the world to go to his clinic. You scored a hottie, girlfriend." Kodi's teasing tone made Reagan blush.

"Fu...dge, did you see that blush? Woo hoo. We're going to have a front seat to this one. Somebody order a case of popcorn and soda." Savannah did a little happy dance in place, making the others giggle.

"Good save on the cursing. Your Master is making progress. But consider yourself forewarned; Masters are sneaky. They'll bait you then paddle you when you mess up. God knows mine are straight up evil when it comes to that trick." Kodi smiled, but Reagan noticed it didn't reach the pretty woman's eyes.

"When is your next book coming out? I'd be happy to beta read for you." Tally's laughter gave away the fact her offer wasn't entirely benevolent.

"You just want to know what happens with the East twins...not fooling me this time, girlfriend."

"Dammit. Those cliff-hangers are just plain mean, Kodi." Tally's lip was pressed out so far in her mock pout Reagan wanted to warn her about a pigeon swooping in for a landing.

"Reagan, do you like to read? I have a pretty extensive collection of books I could share."

Reagan felt the heat of another blush work its way over

her cheeks. "I do. And I loved your first book. I'll probably be stuck in my apartment for a couple of days so..." She stopped talking when the other three women burst out laughing.

"Do you really think Rafe is going to let you go back to a freezing apartment?" Tally was looking at her as if she was a dim-wit.

"An *empty*, freezing apartment."

"Kodi, you are going to be in so much trouble." Savannah shook her head at her friend.

"Fuck-a-dilly circus. I forgot." Kodi didn't sound at all repentant, and Reagan wondered what she was up to.

"What do you mean 'empty'?" Reagan heard the squeak in her voice as she tried to hold her panic in check.

The door opened, and Taz stepped into the room, his gaze zeroing in on his wife. "Baby, you are in big trouble." Kodi ducked her head, but not before Reagan saw her sly smile. "Nanna-son is meeting us for dinner, but she's staying at a motel so she won't be around to save you from the punishment you have coming." Kodi's eyes went wide and were suddenly wary. "Oh, baby, you are so very easy to read. Of course, I knew. You thought she would be your get out of jail free card. You forget how well my brother and I know you, baby."

Taz turned to Reagan and smiled. "You look much better today, sweetness. And what my lovely wife wasn't supposed to mention is that we've cleaned out your apartment. Your landlord has no intention of turning on the heat. He was trying to drive you out so he could remodel and rent the space out to skiers."

Reagan felt her stomach drop. "No job. No place to live. What am I going to do?" *How did I fall so far? I tried to do everything right...and still...* The room was starting to spin around her when she felt warm hands close over hers.

"I swear, Kodi, if you weren't pregnant I'd paddle you myself for upsetting her."

"What? I'm not…"

"Of course, you are. The changes in your skin are easy to see." Shifting his gaze to Taz, he smiled. "Congratulations. I'm sure your grandmother is going to tell you the same thing when you see her later, but you should stop and pick up a test on your way out of town."

The whole room erupted into a flurry of happy chaos, and for a few minutes, Reagan forgot about the fact her life was spiraling down so fast she couldn't seem to stop it. Rafe leaned down to whisper against her ear, "I think Taz and Nate knew, but were afraid to trust what they were hearing. They've wanted this for so long they were afraid it was just wishful thinking. But I'm not kidding about the changes in her skin." He brushed away her tears and raised a brow in question.

"I'm so happy for them. I know Kodi was worried this day would never come." She was grateful for their good news for several reasons. The Ledeks were going to be wonderful parents. Reagan saw the way they took care of their employees and the members of the club, and she envied their future children. But she was also happy to have an excuse to cry. Knowing she had nowhere to go was terrifying.

Taz had been hugging his crying wife, but he turned to her so quickly Reagan felt herself tense at his scrutiny. "Sweetness, I said we moved your things. I did not say you have no place to go. Get that out of your head right now."

Nate pulled Kodi into his arms and kissed her before smiling at Reagan. "That's not how we take care of our friends, Reagan. You should know us better than that by now. We'll let Rafe explain. I'd like to get that test and hit the road. Being late to dinner with Nanna-son isn't an option. And remember, we're going to need you full-time now more than ever."

"Oh yes, please. I really do need you, also. When you see my office and the mess I've made of my social media accounts and advertising, you'll understand why I'm so desperate." Kodi's tear-stained face was filled with such joy Reagan couldn't do anything but nod. Their friendship humbled her, and seeing their happiness made her heart clench with longing.

After the room emptied, the silence was almost deafening. Reagan had realized she'd become increasingly reclusive after the attack, but she hadn't fully understood how much it had affected her until now. Everyone assumed the attack had been the worst part of trauma she'd endured, but it wasn't. The betrayal of trust had hurt more than any of the knife wounds. Knowing the officers charged with her safety cowed to pressure from the Major and administration had cut her to the bone. Pulling in a deep breath, Reagan pushed the pain aside. Until that moment, she hadn't realized Rafe was still standing beside her bed.

RAFE WATCHED EMOTIONS chase over Reagan's face and wondered what it would take to make her feel safe again. She seemed to recognize the fact she was physically safe, but the damage to her soul was going to be much harder to heal. Since his first conversation with Nate, Rafe had spoken with Taz, as well as Kent and Kyle West. The more he learned about Dick Merrett, the more contempt he had for the son of a bitch whose relentless pursuit of Reagan had terrified the young physician's assistant. She'd lost everything in the aftermath. Her friends had abandoned her when she'd refused to stop fighting a battle she couldn't win. She'd been forced to give up the career she loved when the review board in Texas sided with the Department of Corrections staff and pulled her license for "unspecified reasons." What the fuck did that even mean?

Rafe had already contacted the physicians she'd worked for in Texas. Luckily, Kirk Evans and Brian Bennett were members of the Prairie Winds Club, so they'd understood exactly what Rafe meant when he'd said Reagan was *his*. He'd also enlisted help from Sage Morgan, whose political clout in Montana would go a long way to persuading the local board to review her case. Once she'd gotten her license in one state, others would follow suit. Empowering Reagan would help her heal.

"You didn't ask them where they moved your things, Peach." He wanted to chuckle when her eyes widened in realization.

"Oh fudgesicles. I got so caught up in their happiness I forgot. I can get the name of the storage facility later, I guess. Boy, oh boy, I sure hope it's climate controlled. But that means it'll probably be expensive. Shoot, I'd better call Nate or Taz and find out. I don't really have the money to spend on a storage unt…well, unless they'll let me live in it, too. Aside from a bathroom, it probably wouldn't be that bad." She was rambling, and Rafe found himself smiling at the randomness of her thinking.

"Peach, our friends moved your things to my house. The guys moved everything, and the ladies unpacked what they could into your suite. The rest has been stored in the basement for you." He saw her lips part, but didn't wait for her to argue before shaking his head. "Don't start. You need a place to stay, and I will appreciate the company. You'll also be a wonderful house sitter when I have to return to the west coast in a few days." He was pleased to see something close to regret flash in her eyes when he mentioned leaving.

"As much as I know I should protest, I'm too grateful to put up any real fuss." Relief swept through him, and suddenly, he couldn't wait to get her discharged and back in his home. The lacerations on her back and legs were healing quickly, and there was no reason to wait.

"Perfect. I'll finish up your discharge paperwork, and we'll be on our way within the hour." He had big plans for her once they were home. He'd seen the desire in her eyes when she didn't think he was looking, and it matched his own. They were several days past what he'd originally planned, but that didn't mean he was giving up.

Rafe would need to be careful with her, but he could still show her some of the mind-bending pleasure of BDSM. He wanted to spend quality time with Reagan before he was forced to return to San Francisco—he needed to know if his instincts were right about her. And she needed to know whether or not the lifestyle was for her. He'd seen the longing in her eyes when she watched her friends with their Masters. The tighter they held their spirited subs in check, the more intent Reagan's observation.

Reagan appeared to crave structure and a sense of belonging. Things, according to her file, she'd never had as a kid. Those who'd packed up her small apartment reported a small stash of erotic romance novels. They'd sent him a list of the well-worn paperbacks, and he'd noticed a recurring theme when he'd researched the titles.

None of the books were hardcore, but all contained bondage and spanking scenes. Her interest in the lifestyle proved how good her instincts were. She would likely find the sense of security she sought—if she could surrender herself into the care of an experienced Dominant who understood what a treasured gift her submission was.

The nurse told him she'd gotten a quick look at her back, and that she hadn't understood what she'd seen. His patients were always surprised when they saw how quickly they healed. The body could do remarkable things when its wounds were closed properly.

Rafe completed the paperwork in record time and was pleased to see Reagan dressed and ready to leave when he returned to her room. Her uniform had been shredded and discarded the night she was admitted. He'd been more than happy to choose something for her to wear home. The only indication she wasn't pleased with the clothing he'd left for her was the frown lines between her brows. Smart girl that she was, Reagan would wait until she was out the door to voice her complaints.

Chapter Nine

NO PANTIES OR bra. The man had given her a dress that buttoned down the front and a pair of slip on shoes. Okay, so she was grateful the shoes didn't require her to bend over and the dress was easy to put on without moving her arms a lot...but still. She wasn't about to say anything until they were in the car. It would be her luck he would leave her there if she protested too loudly. She didn't want to see the inside of another hospital as a patient for a very long time.

Rafe helped her from the wheelchair, and she stared at the plush towel covering the passenger seat. When she looked at him, the sly smile on his face sent a rush of moisture to her sex. His focus on her was so intense she could almost feel the heat of his stare. "You said you wanted to learn more about the lifestyle, Peach. I will begin as I intend to go." He helped her into the seat and pulled the safety belt over her. "As soon as the door is closed, spread your knees as far apart as you can. Pull the dress up so your pussy is open and available to my touch. I'll usually ask you to pull your dress out from under your pretty ass, but I know that would be too difficult today."

"Holy hat racks." He almost missed her whispered words, and he had to fight to hold back his smile.

"No, Peach. The proper response is 'Yes, Sir.'" She

nodded her head, but he didn't move. When understanding flashed in her eyes, he appreciated the small bit of progress.

"Yes, Sir."

"Good girl. I'm going to enjoy the ride home, immensely. And I intend to make sure you enjoy it, also. Now, remember what you've been instructed to do when the door closes. No need to rack up any punishment points when there are so many more pleasurable ways for us to spend our time together." Damn, he loved watching her eyes widen in surprise a split second before they flamed with yearning. She was going to be a joy to train. No pretension, just raw desire. Smart, beautiful, and—unless he missed his guess—her contained exterior hid a deep well of sensuality.

Closing the door, Rafe watched in his peripheral vision as she shifted in the seat. As her surgeon, he'd already seen every inch of her, but this was something altogether different. This was a Dom getting his first intimate look at his submissive. Settling into the driver's seat, Rafe glanced over at Reagan and smiled. "That's a beautiful blush, sweetheart. I can't remember that last time I saw a woman blush such a lovely shade." She turned positively crimson, and Rafe chuckled.

"What if someone on the second floor looks down? Won't you be embarrassed?"

What? She's worried about my reputation and not her own?

Taking a deep breath, Rafe shook his head. "First of all, I'd never risk embarrassing you in public—well, more specifically, a public venue that wasn't related to the lifestyle. There are often parties for people who are likeminded, and those are considered public. But that's not what we're talking about here." Reaching up, he smoothed the pads of his fingers over her heated cheek. "A Dom's number one priority is seeing to the safety of the submissive in his care. Exposing you to scrutiny would not be in your best interest. I'd never knowingly risk your safety or happiness, Reagan."

"Thank you, but…"

"No, Peach. There is no *but*. You've agreed to try, and I've agreed to teach you. That agreement comes with several implied covenants, the first being that I'll take care of you in all ways possible." He hated the uncertainty he saw in her eyes. Damn, he'd love to kick the ass of whoever made her feel unworthy.

"If you have staff privileges…well, I know how easy it is to have your reputation damaged beyond redemption."

Rafe reached over and pulled her hand to his lips, pressing a kiss to her palm before laying her hand over his heart. Her worry for him was one of the sweetest things anyone had done for him in a very long time. "I'm touched beyond words by your concern, Peach. But I assure you it's not necessary. Now, all this being said…I'll point out that the windows of this SUV don't allow casual observance. That was done intentionally. I hoped to find a submissive of my own someday."

Damn, the woman had the most expressive face he'd ever seen. He hoped she never lost that spark of innocence. "You are the first woman to sit in that seat, Peach. So wipe that insecurity right out of your mind—it has no place between us." If Rafe had his way, there would be nothing between them. He wanted to know everything about her, and the realization surprised him. He'd heard Doms droll on about the importance of complete transparency, but he'd never understood the significance until now.

Vulnerability wouldn't be easy for Reagan. Anyone who'd experienced betrayal to the degree she had would find it difficult to fully lower the shields around their heart. But the more time he spent with her, the more interested Rafe was in helping her move past the pain.

Leaning over the console, Rafe brushed a quick kiss over her lips. He'd deliberately kept the contact brief because anything more substantial would snap his control and he'd end up making out with her in the damned hospital parking lot like a randy teenager. "We need to go, or I'm going to risk both our reputations and strip that dress from you and feast on your beasts until you come screaming my name."

Rafe didn't wait for her response. Turning his attention to driving, he maneuvered the SUV out through the streets at the edge of town, taking in the landscape. It was remarkable how much the area around the medical center was changing. Ryan Morgan was working hard to make the hospital into one of the most progressive in the region, but it was his wife who'd put the small city's facility on the map. Joelle Phillips Morgan's Nobel Prize winning cancer research and her connections in the world of pharmaceuticals made it possible for her to build a state of the art research center adjacent to the hospital. The Morgan Health Care Foundation operated both facilities and was creating serious buzz in the medical and research communities around the world.

When he saw her inching her legs closer together, Rafe decided it was time to up the stakes. "Leave your legs open, Peach. All the way open and unbutton all but the top button on your dress." He frowned at her when she hesitated and was pleased to see her scramble to do as she'd been told. "Very good. I want to see you, Peach. Tell me, is your pussy wet for me?"

Reagan sucked in a breath before quietly whispering,

"Yes, Sir."

"Perfect. Lean your seat back, Peach. I want to play with you. I've wanted to slide my fingers through the slick folds between your thighs since the first time I saw you. The snug, well-worn denim jeans you wore molded to your ass so perfectly they could have been painted on. The only flaw in the picture was the line from your panties. That won't be a problem for you while we're together. Remember, this lovely body is mine to enjoy."

She gave him a questioning look, and he grinned. "Ask the other subs at the club if their Masters allow them to wear panties." He'd intentionally used the term Masters rather than Doms to see if she would object to his subtle claim and was pleased when she didn't protest. "I assure you they are rarely allowed to wear the offensive undergarments. I doubt they put up much of a fuss since most are tired of having their expensive lingerie shredded when their Master or Mistresses rips them off."

"Well, I don't really have any pretty things left, so that won't really be an issue for me." He didn't bother to tell her the ladies who'd helped unpack her clothes had thrown out more than they'd kept. They'd insisted her wardrobe was in such poor condition they'd known he would want to replace it. *Sneaky subs.*

"I can smell your sweet cream, Peach. It's making me hard as a fucking hammer. Use your left hand to slide your fingers through the petals. Get your fingers nice and wet."

"Now? Here?" And there was the resistance he'd been expecting.

Rafe didn't bother to answer. He just pulled over to the edge of the highway and put the transmission in park. "That will cost you five swats when you're healed enough to take them. Would you like to add to that tally or are you going to follow the order you were given?"

Reagan's eyes went wide, and her eyes darted left and right before her hand slowly slipped to the juncture of her thighs. "Had you followed the instruction immediately, you'd have saved yourself a spanking. Also, you could have done this same thing without my complete attention. But then I'd have missed the spectacular way your folds are flowering open as more blood flows to your pussy. And I wouldn't have been able to watch your fingers slide deep or hear the sound of your wet pussy as it sucks the slender digits deeper."

He'd only planned to have her play with her wet labia enough to get her fingers wet before pulling them to his mouth. But now, he was going to use this as a teachable moment. He watched her fingers moving slowly from the opening of her vagina to just above her clit in unpracticed moves, and he wondered how much experience she had with self-pleasure. Most women her age had enough previous experience to zero in on a particular spot using practiced movements that gave them the most pleasure. Reagan wasn't doing, either; her movements were haphazard at best.

"How often do you masturbate, Reagan?" She gasped and started shaking her head. "Let me rephrase the question. When is the last time you had an orgasm?" This time, she dropped her chin to her chest, but not before he saw her eyes fill with tears. Using one hand to still her frantic movements chafing her now dry sex, he gently pushed her hand aside and replaced it with his own. Then he used the other hand to tilt her face to his. "I'm going to make you come, Peach. We aren't going to waste any time because we're on the side of the road, but you need this, and I'm going to make sure you get it. Keep your eyes on my face, Peach. No matter what happens, you keep your eyes on my face. Do you understand?"

Her voice was shaky, but the words were quick. "Yes, Sir."

"Perfect. You are so responsive. You're already wet for me. Feel how easily my fingers slide along the slick folds? That's it, sweetheart. Suck in those deep breaths. Send all that oxygen flowing into your body. It'll fuel your orgasm and make you fly higher. Come as soon as you're ready." With the last words, he pushed two fingers deep into her hot channel and began fucking her with fast strokes that skimmed her G-spot on each thrust.

"You're so close, baby. I can feel your vaginal walls trembling around my fingers. I can hardly wait to slide my cock into your tight pussy." Her body vibrated with the need for release, but something was holding her back. Taking a chance, he moved his hand from her chin to the tightly peaked nipple nearest him and gave it a sharp pinch. The bite of pain was all it took to send her flying. "Fuck yeah. Your cream just soaked my fingers. Come all over my hand, baby. Juicy as a sweet peach. I knew you would be."

She'd gasped out his name before biting down so hard on her lip to keep from screaming it was a wonder she hadn't broken the skin. When her body stopped convulsing around his fingers, he reluctantly pulled them free, sucking them into his mouth and moaning in pleasure. He loved watching her eyes go wide with surprise. *Hasn't any man ever savored her release?* Her flavor burst over his tongue, making him wish he could bury his face between her thighs and see how many times he could make her come before she begged for mercy.

Pulling a soft throw from the backseat, he covered her sweat-sheened body. "Close your eyes and rest, Peach. We'll be home before you know it." He'd barely gotten back up to speed on the highway before he heard her respiration settle into the slow, even pattern of sleep. His cock was throbbing with an aching desire to find his own release, but he still found himself oddly satisfied. Reagan might not realize it, but they'd just had their first scene as a D/s couple. And, rather than planning his exit strategy, he was anxious to getting her back home and wrap himself around her naked body. Holding her while she slept would help them build trust and he looked forward to the intimacy of feeling her naked skin pressed against his own.

Rafe was grateful for the few minutes of quiet. He used the time to re-center himself and regain control of his libido. *Damn, no woman has ever tested me like this. What the fuck?* Everything about Reagan flipped his switches, and seeing her come around his fingers made his balls feel like they were filled with molten lava. He couldn't remember the last time he'd almost come in his damned jeans. Shaking his head, Rafe turned off the highway. Taking a sanded backroad, he pulled into his garage a few minutes later. After killing the engine and closing the outside door, he turned to the sleeping angel in the passenger seat. Watching the rhythmic rise and fall of Reagan's chest as she slept filled him with an unfamiliar sense of peace.

The dark circles under eyes had faded a small degree, but he wanted to see them disappear altogether before he returned to the coast. He'd briefly considered taking her with him, but he'd been sure Reagan would be anxious to start working again. Her work ethic impressed him as much as it frustrated him. *Just let me take care of you for a couple of days, sweetheart. Put yourself in my care, and I promise I won't let you down.*

Chapter Ten

KELSEY HUNG UP the phone and shuddered. It had taken a couple of days of phone tag before she'd been able to talk to the man Reagan called Major Asshole. But it had only taken her a few seconds to figure out the jerk certainly deserved the nickname. Arrogant didn't even begin to cover it. He'd been both egotistical and condescending; clearly, the man was used to barking orders and having them followed without question. She'd played at Mountain Mastery enough to know the difference between a sexual Dominant and an abusive prick, and Dick Merrett was the latter.

He'd been steadfast in his refusal to pay her for information. "Why would I pay you to find out the location of a disgraced employee? If Reagan is involved in something illegal, you should probably contact your local authorities. I'd be happy to do that for you if you'll just tell me where she is." The bastard wanted the information for free. When she'd asked him why he wasn't willing to pay her, he'd laughed. "You didn't do your homework very well, did you? I have two kids in college and an ex-wife from hell. I don't have ten grand lying around. Just because I'm the third in command of this facility doesn't mean they pay me what I'm worth." He'd then proceeded to badger her about Reagan's location for so long she'd finally disconnected the call.

Leaning back against her new leather sofa, Kelsey skimmed her hand back and forth over the supple surface and let the call replay in her mind. She'd given him a fictitious name, but he'd called her Kelsey just before she'd disconnected the call...the realization sent chills up her spine. He'd kept her on the phone long enough to trace the call. No wonder he'd stalled so long on the phone. The bastard had probably recorded their conversation as well. That would explain why everything he'd said sounded so...cautious.

Kelsey should warn Reagan, but how would she explain how she'd learned the other woman was in danger? Reagan might be a sucker when it came to doing someone else's work, but she certainly wasn't stupid. There was no way Kelsey would emerge from that conversation unscathed. *It's not like Rafe is going to let me near her anyway.* Kelsey had heard Reagan was injured at Mountain Mastery, but she didn't know if the other woman was back in her tiny apartment. If not, getting through Ryan Morgan or Rafe standing guard at the hospital would be virtually impossible.

She couldn't call Master Nate or Master Taz at the club. Either one of them would recognize her voice. And the rumors she'd heard about them reading minds made her more than a little nervous. There wasn't any reason to find out whether or not those stories were true. Her only option was to notify the local authorities. She could block the caller I.D. on her phone and tell Sheriff Brandt Morgan. She'd seen him a few times, but had never talked to him, so there wasn't any chance he'd recognize her voice.

Taking a deep breath, Kelsey scribbled out what she wanted to say on a piece of scrap paper. After revising is several times, she'd finally worked up the courage to make the call.

SHAKING HIS HEAD, Brandt Morgan stared at his laptop screen and wondered why Kelsey Jones was trying to conceal her identity. When the dispatcher sent the call through to his office, she'd noted the caller I.D. was blocked and the young woman on the other end wouldn't give her name. Unfortunately for Kelsey, Brandt's younger brother was one of the most talented computer security programmers in the country. Phoenix had made certain Brandt's office was equipped with enough technology to ensure he was always certain who he was talking to and exactly where the caller was located.

With the press of a few keys, Brandt easily tagged Kelsey's phone. He'd be able to follow her for twenty-four hours before he needed to take the matter to a judge to continue monitoring her. Granted, he wasn't exactly coloring inside the lines, but considering the bull shit happening in Washington, he wasn't too worried. The news coming out of that swamp was making it more and more difficult to stomach television.

He listened as she stumbled through her story. It was obvious she was reading from notes, which made him even more curious about what she was hiding. Brandt marveled at her claim a man she knew was a threat to a former coworker had called her but hadn't known her name. *How stupid does she think I am?* He'd bet his interest in hell she'd hoped for a payday in return for information about Reagan's location, but obviously, the man hadn't been interested in shelling out any money. Considering his position in the Department of Corrections, he'd likely discovered who he was talking to and where she was within seconds of answering the call.

It didn't take a rocket scientist to figure out the only reason she was calling him now was because she was worried the jerk was going to show up without coughing up any money. Since most of Rafe Newell's stalking issues with Kelsey had been in San Francisco, Brandt had never spoken to her. But from everything he'd heard, the woman was a real piece of work.

When she finally stopped stuttering through the bull shit story she'd been trying to feed him, Brandt opened his mouth to ask her the first of several obvious questions. Much to his frustration, all he heard was dead air. *I fucking hate it when people hang up on me.*

Brandt sent a quick message to Phoenix asking for information about Kelsey Jones, including a full report on her financial status. Her call had tripped all his internal alarms, and as a former SEAL, he had been trained to never ignore his gut. Phoenix's response flashed on his screen almost immediately and made Brandt smile.

She's a nut-job. San Francisco cops didn't charge her because they'd been assured she was coming back here and would be your problem. If I get you the info, you have to promise to lock her up or send her packing.

Brandt chuckled to himself at his brother's response. Phoenix was considered the most even-keeled of the five Morgan brothers, so his terse reply was amusing. It wasn't difficult to see who'd been up with baby last night. Phoenix's wife, Aspen, had joined the Prairie Winds team and was currently on the other side of the world helping rescue a kidnapping victim, leaving her two husbands with a very vocal toddler. Little Athena Morgan was hell on wheels. She'd come crashing into the world a month early and had been running the show ever since. Like her Greek Goddess namesake, Athena manipulated her parents like chess pieces.

Hearing the door open, Brandt turned to see his beautiful wife step into the room. Without bothering to greet him, she turned back to the door and flipped the lock in place. Letting the long trench coat she wore slip down her arms, she set it aside and turned. Fucking hell, the dress she was wearing was molded to her so perfectly it looked more like a second skin. Her nipples were drawn into tight little peaks, and when her gaze locked with his, it was blazing with desire.

"To what do I owe this unexpected pleasure, Minx?" Joelle's eyes flashed with challenge, and Brandt smiled to himself. *Bring it, sweetheart. I'm all about this game.* She owned him in ways he couldn't explain. Her love had pulled him out of a downward PTSD spiral that had terrified his own family. Brilliant, beautiful, and a heart as pure as any he'd ever known—and she was his.

"I've missed you." Brandt translated the words mentally—his wife was horney and she'd come to him. *Perfect.*

"Have you now? What makes you think it's okay to show up unannounced at my office dressed in a knit dress that someone painted on you? You're not wearing anything under that tight dress are you, minx?"

She was still standing across the room from him, but Brandt swore he saw her nipples draw up tighter and heard her soft gasp. He gave her a knowing smile when she shifted to rub her legs together. "It won't work you know—you can slide those lovely thighs together all day long and it won't relieve the ache. Your Masters are the only ones who can quench that need, minx."

The blush staining her cheeks sent a surge of blood to his cock. He'd never get tired of seeing the innocence in her eyes. He and Ryan had introduced her to ménage and been thrilled at how perfectly suited she was to their lifestyle. Their demanding jobs made sharing a wife the perfect solution. Now that Ryan's duties at the hospital were expanding, he was working more, leaving Joelle home alone more than they'd like. But hopefully, that wouldn't last much longer. The additional staff the health foundation hired would soon be in place. Brandt was grateful because he missed having her naked between them. Joelle's response to double penetration ménage was something to behold.

Letting his gaze slide down her lush body like a heated caress, Brandt wanted to fist pump at her response. A shudder worked its way to the surface of her eyes, their pupils dilated until nothing but a narrow ring of their brilliant green remained. And those candy pink nipples that always tasted so sweet? They were tight points that threatened to poke through the loosely woven knit fabric of her dress. *Stunning. Horney. Mine.*

"Strip." Living up to her nickname, the little minx taunted him by slowly slipping the boots from her feet before pulling the dress over her head. Just as he'd suspected, she hadn't worn a stitch of clothing underneath. She'd lost the weight she'd gained while pregnant, but their child had left her mark on her mama's gorgeous body. Brandt and Ryan both relished each of those fading stretchmarks; they were proof of the gift she'd given them.

Turning his chair, he crooked his finger, calling her to stand between his spread legs. "You are so fucking beautiful. You take my breath away." When she dropped her eyes, he refused to let her hide in shame. "No, minx. Look at me. Ry and I are going to keep telling you until you believe every word. Your body *has* changed, but we both feel blessed by those changes. If anything, we want you more now than we did before, and I'd have sworn to you that wouldn't be possible."

Skimming his hands up her outer thighs, Brand followed the path north until they spanned her narrow waist, his thumbs resting over her taut abdomen. "It's hard to believe there was a beautiful baby in here not so long ago. No one has ever given me a more precious gift."

"You and Master Ryan gave me the gift to begin with. I just nurtured the seed." Tears filled her eyes, but she blinked them back. "Your acceptance of the changes in my body make me love you even more. You're very good for my self-esteem." Her words hit him right in the center of his chest—his heart skipped a beat at their sincerity. *Maybe we're starting to get through to her.*

"We'll never lie to you. We promised you that in the beginning. That isn't the way you treat people you love and respect." He and Ryan had both sworn to always tell her the truth, no matter how difficult. If they were going to demand transparency from her, they needed to do the same. That's not to say they didn't occasionally tell her they wouldn't answer a question. Some things submissives needed to experience without any time to mentally prepare. And with a sub as smart as theirs, it was even more necessary.

Moving his hands up until they covered her rounded breasts, Brandt caught both nipples between his fingers and gave them a long, slow pinch. Her knees wobbled and caught the scent of her sweet cream. "Such a good girl. Are you wet for me, minx?"

"Yes, Sir."

Fuck, the woman was so perfect there were times he still couldn't believe she was theirs. Moving his fingers slowly down to the cream coating her pussy lips, he was thrilled to see her legs already sliding farther apart. Slipping the calloused tips of his fingers between the soaking wet folds, Brandt pressed his lips against her quivering stomach. "Fuck, you are drenched, minx. You have no idea how much it turns me on to know your body is ready for me."

When he finally slipped his fingers into her sheath, zeroing in on her sweet spot, Joelle's knees started to shake, making him chuckle. "Not yet, minx." Regretfully, he pulled his fingers free and licked them clean. Watching heat flame in her eyes as she observed him savor the tangy flavor of her arousal. "Over my knees, minx. I'm going to give you a spanking we're both going to enjoy."

Without hesitation, Joelle draped herself over his lap. She loved erotic spankings, the edge of pain ramping her body up quickly. She'd obviously missed the intimacy of being over his and Ryan's knees—something they'd denied her since learning she was pregnant. After she'd given birth, Ryan had insisted her body needed time to heal, so this was the first time in over a year Brandt had gotten to feel her lying over his thighs pressing against his raging hard-on. The position was perfect, but definitely a mixed blessing. *Jesus, Joseph, and Mary, I've missed this.* The first heated caress took her by surprise; her shriek made him grin. "If you don't want everyone in the office to know what's happening, you'd better hold it down, minx." He spread the next swats over her curved cheeks, loving the blush chasing his warm hand.

He wasn't going to tell her the only one who'd be able to hear her was his new deputy, Lee Barber. There was a shared wall and a small Jack and Jill bathroom between their offices. Brandt smiled to himself. Lee was a sexual Dominant and member of Mountain Mastery, so he'd know exactly what was going on.

And right on cue, Brandt's phone chimed. The incoming message from Lee flashed on the screen. *Fuck you, boss. How am I supposed to work with that going on next door? Heading out on patrol.* Brandt grinned, but didn't respond to the message. He wasn't about to interrupt a scene with the gorgeous woman lying over his lap to text.

He could feel her soaking the leg of his uniform pants and grinned to himself knowing he'd have to change before leaving for the day. Brandt landed one last swat before pushing his fingers into her and whispering the words she was unconsciously waiting to hear. "Come for me, minx." Her body reacted before he'd even finished speaking. Joelle's vaginal muscles clamped down tight, milking his fingers as they tried to pull him deeper into her sheath.

Lifting her, Brandt laid her over the desk and took a steadying breath. "I'm going to fuck you, minx. This is going to be hard and fast."

"Yes. Please. Sir." Her voice was strained, and he wasn't about to let her down.

"We'll do slow and sweet later. Right now, I need you too damned bad to hold back." He had his pants open, and his unsheathed cock at her opening by the time he stopped speaking. With one flex of his hips, Brandt buried himself balls deep and cursed. "Fucking hell, your pussy is still flexing from your climax. You're stealing every last shred of my control. Hold on."

Long, hard strokes at a brutal pace sent them both over the edge in record time. It was over too soon, but each time the head of his cock connected with her cervix, he felt her spasm around him. The intensity of his release made his knees buckle. Falling over her, Brandt was grateful he'd managed most of his weight on his forearms.

"Fuck me. You undo me every time, minx. But this? This was soul-stealing." He'd taken her without protection, but the Neanderthal in him wanted to roar and beat his chest. Deep inside, he was certain he'd just given her another child to nurture, and he could hardly wait to find out if he was right.

"I promise to move as soon as I can trust my legs, minx."

"No hurry. I'm done in. I may just spend the night right here. The door's locked so we'll call it good."

"Not happening, my love. I promised you slow and sweet, and I intend to deliver as soon as we deliver our little princess to the ranch." His sister in law, Coral, was having an overnight party for all the kids and Ryan was working late, so it was going to be his first evening alone with his wife in several weeks. He intended to enjoy it!

Chapter Eleven

"WAKE UP, SLEEPYHEAD. We're home." Rafe had opened her door and leaned down beside Reagan, hoping to minimize any startle reflex. Sudden movements would cause discomfort for a couple of days, so he planned to wake her slowly. "Open those gorgeous brown eyes for me, Peach. I'd carry you inside but you wouldn't enjoy the pressure on your back and legs." It could rip open several of the deeper wounds, but he didn't see any reason to be quite that graphic.

She blinked her eyes and gave him a lopsided grin. "I wouldn't want you to undo all Dr. Newell's fancy repair work. He's a famous plastic surgeon, you know. I'm very swank to have been his patient." He wanted to laugh out loud at her faux awe. Damn, he was pleased she was showing him a glimpse of the real woman behind the stoic mask she'd maintained with the hospital staff. Ryan had even tried shuffling the nursing staff so her attendants were more her age, but it hadn't mattered. Reagan had been unfailingly polite, but she'd kept everyone at arm's length.

Before her eyelids could, once again, flutter closed, Rafe took her small hand and pulled her slowly to her feet. His cock stirred at the feeling of his much larger hand wrapped around her slender fingers. She blinked at him a few times as if trying to bring him into focus, and he grinned when little frown lines appeared between her brows. "It's not a good idea to frown at your Master, Peach."

"Then stand still. You keep weaving around, and I can't get a bead on you."

"You make it sound as if you're going to shoot me."

"Oh, heaven's no. Why would I shoot someone who gives earth shattering orgasms on the fly? All those fast food joints are going to have to go a long way to top your *to-go service*."

Rafe couldn't hold back his laughter as they walked into the house. When he stopped, she glanced up at him in question. Damn, he loved that befuddled expression. He dropped her hand and released the last remaining button of the dress she was wearing, enjoying her quick inhalation. "I want to see you. More often than not, I'll want you naked when we are alone." He used his fingers to lift her face to his before continuing. "You know Masters love to show off their submissives at the club, too. I'm going to love showing you off, Peach."

He saw a myriad of emotions in her eyes. But the one he was going to deal with first was the shadow of shame. "Be very careful, Reagan. I'll take offense at anything negative you say about yourself. Be sure…be very sure you're prepared to go down that path before you speak." She pulled her bottom lip between her teeth, and he could practically hear the wheels spinning in her mind, but she remained silent. *Good enough for now*.

Slipping the garment from her shoulders, he smoothed his palms down her ribs and hummed when her nipples tightened into tight points. "You are gorgeous, Peach. I can hardly wait to share our second scene."

"Second? Scene?" There was that confused look he was

coming to love.

Giving her nipples a quick squeeze to center her attention, he nodded. "Don't doubt for a minute what you experienced on our way here was a scene. I gave commands. You obeyed. And you were rewarded with the release your body was craving and needed to shut down that quick mind of yours and get a few minutes rest." The surprise was easy to see in her expression. "Scenes don't have to be elaborate productions, Peach."

"But how will I know if it's a scene? What if we're talking and you decide to start a scene? I might not realize it….and I'll mess up. I've seen how that works out for subs at the club…and it's never good. You have to know I'll mess up…I'm always misjudging people."

Jesus, she was sliding into a full-blown panic attack simply because she was worried about making a mistake. She hadn't said anything about being afraid of punishments. She was solely focused on her fear of displeasing him.

"Stop. Hell, baby, take a breath." Once she seemed to have come back a step or two from the edge, he led her to the living room. Sitting in one of the oversized recliners, he settled her on his lap and pulled her into his arms. He didn't want to have this conversation in the bedroom because he felt strongly about making sure that space was reserved for sleep and sex—and not necessarily in that order.

"First of all, rest assured I'll never hold you responsible for a rule you didn't know. They call it training for a reason, Peach. This lifestyle can be complicated, but it's just like everything else. You'll learn it one step at a time. I know you already understand the importance of following orders." Nate and Taz included the basics of BDSM play in their employee training program. "And, you're already familiar with the club's safe words since it's an important part of every employee's orientation, so we'll use the same stoplight system here. If we keep it consistent, you won't have to think about where you are and what word you should use."

Her breathing was slowly returning to normal, and the pulse at the base of her neck was no longer racing. "I'm sorry. I didn't mean to lose it. It's just that, well, I don't like to make mistakes. When you mess up, people stop loving...I mean, they stop liking you. And then you have to move on and..."

Rafe put his finger over her lips, silencing her. He wasn't about to let her finish, because that line of thinking had no place between them.

"Stop. That's not the way it works, Peach. Not at Mountain Mastery and certainly not with me." He could see the doubt in her eyes and realized he needed to find another approach. It was abundantly clear she'd never had anyone she could depend on past the first mistake. He couldn't even imagine what that would be like to have people in his life who bailed at the first sign of trouble.

"Do you abandon your friends the first time they make a mistake?" Her thunderous expression almost made him laugh. Here was a woman who was fiercely loyal to the people she valued. Knowing she'd be equally faithful to a lover sent heat coursing through his veins.

"No, of course not."

"But you think I would?" Her eyes widened before they dropped to where her hands were twisting in her lap. "Look at me, Peach." Her face slowly lifted back to his, and he saw the sheen of tears in her eyes. "I'm loyal to my friends, too, Reagan. I'll be even more devoted to the woman who entrusts me with her body. I'll cherish that gift, baby. But I also understand trust is built over time."

The first tears breached her lower lids and raced down her chin. Leaning forward, Rafe kissed the salty drops away and then rested his forehead against hers. "One step at a time, Peach. I promise to take this one step at a time. But I want something from you in return. I want you to promise to tell me if you're feeling insecure or if something we're doing frightens you. Relationships in the BDSM world are almost always stronger than those of our vanilla counterparts because communication is such a huge part of what we do. You'll never be punished for asking a question—as long as you do so respectfully."

He saw her sag in relief and took that as his cue to move things along. Setting her up on her feet, he stood and pressed a kiss to her forehead. "Come on. I'm beat. Ryan is going to have to do something about the deplorable conditions of the doctor's lounge if he expects me to work out of that facility. Swear to God, I'll build my own wing if that's what it takes to get a decent nap. I'm certain their mattresses are something they picked up at a five and dime store."

Reagan's giggle made froze him in his tracks. When he turned, her eyes widened in concern. "What? Did I do something wrong?"

"No, Peach. Quite the contrary. I think that's the sweetest sound I've ever heard. I'm going to make it my goal to hear it as often as possible." This time his lips locked on hers and went from chaste to scorching in a heartbeat. When he finally made himself pull back, they were both panting. "Fucking hell. You undo me."

Rafe was leading her down the hallway toward the master suite when she suddenly stopped. "This isn't the way to the room where I left my overnight bag."

Facing her, Rafe cradled her face between his large hands. "No, it isn't. I know I told you that you could have your own room. Is that what you want, Peach? Or would you rather sleep in my arms?"

REAGAN WAS SO surprised by Rafe's question she couldn't do anything except blink her eyes as she tried to wrap her mind around the implications. He hadn't said anything about sex. Had he changed his mind? Maybe her insecurities were too much of a turn off? Or maybe he only wanted her to sleep beside him in case any medical issues came up during the night?

"Peach? I asked you a question, and I expect an answer. You're overthinking this. I can see it playing out in your eyes. Make no mistake, I want to fuck you so badly my dick feels like it's seconds away from exploding." Her eyes dropped to where his cock strained against the denim of his jeans. "Yes, take a good look, Peach. That's what you do to me. But I'm not ruled by lust. You and I are both exhausted. We need sleep, and that's what we're going to do. Holding you will help me sleep, and I think it will help you, too."

She nodded, her mind numb, and the reality of her situation started to sink in. This man wasn't asking for anything except the opportunity to hold her as she slept. No one had done that since she was a small child. Her body reacted before her mind realized she was moving. Reagan stepped forward to lay her cheek against Rafe's chest and wrapped her arms around his waist. "I'd like that very much. You're right. I'm tired, and I can't imagine how spent you must be."

Relief swept through her when he closed his arms around her. The hug was comforting rather than sexual, and that was enough to calm her fears. She hadn't had sex with anyone in a very long time, and the thought of breaking her dry-spell when she was weaving on her feet from fatigue almost sent her into a tail-spin. "Come on."

She let him lead her into his bedroom and gasped when she spotted a couple of her dime store trinkets sitting on the bedside table. "Our friends obviously knew I wouldn't want you sleeping anywhere else." She heard the amusement in his voice, but there was a sublayer of affection, too. As he stripped out of his own clothes, Reagan realized for the first time she was naked. Holy cannoli, how had she forgotten she'd been completely bared to his gaze?

She heard him chuckle across the room and looked up to see him watching her. "Just realized you weren't wearing anything, didn't you?"

"Yes. I can't believe I forgot."

"For what it's worth, I'm thrilled. That level of comfort tells me a lot." He studied her so intently she wondered if Mountain Mastery was filled with mind-reading Doms. "Sweetheart, I hope you don't play poker."

What? Poker? "No, I was never very lucky at cards."

Rafe head fell back as he laughed. Reagan might have been insulted if the sound of his hearty laugh wasn't so genuine. "No, Peach. Luck has very little to do with success in poker, but that wasn't what I was referring to. I meant you don't have a poker face. Nothing is hidden. Your honest emotions are a siren's call to a Dom like me."

Reagan tilted her head to the side, trying to make sense of what he was saying, but she was just too tired to sort through it. Shaking his head, he crossed the distance between them. Walking her backward until she felt the bed behind her, he used a hand on her shoulder to sit her on the edge of the mattress. "Lie back before you fall asleep on your feet. We'll work it all out in the morning."

The light went out a second later, and even though she heard him moving around the bed, she was asleep before he joined her. Somewhere in the back of her mind she realized she was wrapped in warmth and sweet words were being whispered against her ear, but she slid into the darkness before she could make sense of what the words meant.

Chapter Twelve

Koi stood by fireplace in Karl and Tally's home, watching the flames dance over the logs. He'd let himself in a half hour ago, enough time to slip the take-out he'd picked up into the warming oven and start a fire. Karl was in his home office, but the glass door was closed so he hadn't interrupted what sounded like a heated phone conversation. Koi didn't know who the good Senator was talking to, but it was obvious he was pissed as hell about some detail of his upcoming trip. He'd tried to tell Karl it was a fool's venture and entirely too dangerous, but so far, the other man still planned to go.

Tally rushed through the front door, her arms laden with books and bags. Shaking his head, he moved to where she was struggling to slip out of her wet shoes. *"Ma poupée*, why didn't you tell me you had things to carry in? Why must women be so stubborn?"

"Stubborn? Me? Surely you jest!" Her laughter filled the room, and Koi found himself laughing along with her. How long had it been since he'd enjoyed a woman's teasing—other than his sister, Kodi, of course? She'd been the light of his life since the moment his parents walked in the front door with her in their arms. Hell, he couldn't even remember the last time he'd enjoyed a casual conversation with a member of the opposite sex.

"She's as stubborn as they come. Never asks for help, even when it's blatantly obvious she needs it." Karl's voice behind Tally made her shriek.

Jumping, she spun around clutching her chest. "Holy fucking hell, you scared ten years off my life."

"And you, my lovely sub, just bought yourself a swat for each of those years. We'll take care of that after dinner. You have five minutes to freshen up. You can begin by stripping here." Koi watched Tally's cheeks flame, but she didn't argue, quickly shedding her clothes and then making her way down the hall. Karl looked at him and grinned. "Damn, she couldn't have set us up any better. I hope like hell she never learns to curb her foul mouth. Although I must admit, lately startling her is about the only way to shake the word 'fuck' out of her."

Koi laughed and shook his head as he carried her packages into the kitchen. Setting everything on the breakfast bar, he started pulling the food from the oven. "Let me guess, she has trouble shedding her independence when you return home."

"That's putting it mildly. Tally is brilliant. Those aren't just the words of a proud husband, either. The woman's I.Q. rivals Phoenix Morgan's. She sailed through school, college, and medical school. She was well on her way to becoming the hottest surgeon in the D.C. metro area when we met. One trip to my home state and she fell in love." Koi could see the regret in Karl's eyes when he quietly added, "I don't know how I'm going to break it to her that she's going to move back."

When a door closed at the end of the hall, Karl shook his head, and Koi let his questions go. If everything he'd heard about Tally was true, it was going to be very difficult for her to fit in with the elitists who controlled the social networking in Washington, D.C. In Koi's experience, those women were ruthless in their exclusivity. They didn't welcome newcomers. Those sharks would scent Tally's inexperience like blood in water. Fuck, they'd shred her until there was nothing left of the wide-eyed beauty who'd just stepped into the kitchen.

Her braided hair and freshly washed face made her appear even younger than she was. His heart clenched thinking about Karl throwing her to the wolves. Koi was aware of Tyson's political aspirations, but he didn't understand why the other man was willing to let his personal ambition trump his wife's happiness. Looking at Karl, Koi nodded to the food he'd set out. "You might want to tie a towel around your lovely sub. Chinese food can be messy, and I'd hate to see her burn those beautiful breasts."

"We'll feed her. It'll be a good chance for her to practice obedience." There was suddenly a thin strain of venom in Karl's voice that set Koi's nerves on edge. Tally was clearly surprised, as well, her eyes widening before dropping to the floor. Koi had been told the Tyson's marriage was rock solid, but he was beginning to wonder how much their mutual friends really knew about Karl and Tally Tyson.

PHOENIX MORGAN STUDIED the video playing on the large monitor in his office then turning his attention to where his brother sat beside him. Brandt swore under his breath, "Fuck. There's not much question what's going on."

"I'd say she's been doing this for a while since she seems to have forgotten about the security cameras."

"She's probably more pressed for time now that she doesn't have Reagan to pawn her work off on. When I interviewed the other employees, almost all of them mentioned Kelsey's ability to shift the burden of her work to her coworker."

"Why didn't any of them speak up?" It was bull shit like this that made Phoenix grateful he'd never worked for anyone other than friends and family. Hell, he didn't even do tech work for anyone he didn't like—he didn't need to.

"They preferred dealing with Reagan. Un-fucking-believable. Selfish bastards claimed they liked Reagan better, and since she was easier for them to deal with, they stood by silently as she did Kelsey's work as well as her own." Brandt sighed and shook his head as he replayed a section of the video. "Serves Kelsey right that she is now doing both jobs alone."

"Actually, being forced to do her own work is probably putting a serious kink in her little enterprise—and not the good kind of kink, either." Phoenix watched as Kelsey scrambled to hide what looked like a boot box when she heard someone approaching.

"I don't want to know how you got this, do I?" Brandt glanced his way, and Phoenix grinned.

"I have a contract to provide technical support for the freight company. I'll claim I was tweaking their system out of the goodness of my heart, and when I discovered her nefarious activities, I contacted the local authorities."

"But no one is going to believe that. Everybody knows you spend every spare minute with my sweet niece or inside your wife."

"Says the pot to the kettle. Can the choirboy bull shit; I already know about your late afternoon visitor yesterday." Phoenix's mocking laughter had Brandt shaking his head.

"Small towns are a pain in the ass."

"Not this time. Joelle called Calamity to babysit, but she was out on a vet call. Caila called Coral, who was in Missoula with Mom. Coral called me looking for Aspen, who is still out of the country." Calamity was the Morgan brothers' nickname for their younger brother Kip's wife, Caila. She'd grown up on the ranch bordering their own and had been considered part of the family long before she'd married the youngest of Dean and Patsy Morgan's five sons. Coral was married to Sage, Brandt's oldest brother. Since Coral had been the first "sister" to join the family, she held a special place in all of their hearts.

"Jesus H. Christ. Who babysat?" Brandt often forgot about the Morgan grapevine even though he'd once sworn even Uncle Sam didn't have a comm system faster than his family's.

"Yours truly. There isn't much I won't do for my sisters-in-law. And, well, Joelle is really special."

Brandt grinned at his brother. "Thanks. She and I needed the time alone. And her visit was a very pleasant surprise. Coral keeping Jezzi overnight was a gift straight from heaven."

Brandt's transparency surprised Phoenix. He seemed amused, but not surprised by the flabbergasted expression on Phoenix's face. Brandt had been an entirely different person after he left the SEALs. His last mission had been a complete cluster fuck—losing so many teammates had decimated him. His physical injuries had healed quickly, but the survivor's guilt and PTSD had steamrolled him. He'd locked himself away in his anger and guilt; in the year before Joelle became a part of his life, he'd alienated his friends and tried desperately to push his family away. But Joelle had changed everything. She'd pulled Brandt from the dark place he'd retreated, and their parents and brothers all worshipped her for it.

"Maybe it would be easier to get the warrant if a small video clip was sent to you anonymously. Hell, if the newspapers in New York and Washington can use anonymous sources, seems only right that you should be able to do the same."

Brandt shook his head and chuckled. "You really need to stay off Twitter."

"Remember, you learn more from people who disagree with you. They force you to think through your opinions."

Brandt moved to the door, still shaking his head. "Another reason you should avoid all social media. You're already too fucking smart for your own good." Phoenix had been hearing that sentiment his entire life, but he'd never been impressed with his Mensa level I.Q. In his opinion, being smart was a small part of the battle. Being smart without being motivated was like owning a fancy car but refusing to put fuel in it.

"Uncle Brandt, you aren't supposed to say that word. Mommy says it's bad. Even Daddy gets in trouble for that, and he's the boss of the whole world." Phoenix grinned at Brandt's contrite expression. There was nothing like being chastised by a four-year-old with the brass of a twenty-four-year old.

"You're right, Charity. I'll try to do better."

"Splendid." Brandt's eyes widened, and it took all Phoenix's control to not laugh out loud. Charity Morgan was already testing off the charts and made her way to Phoenix's office anytime she could give her mother and sisters the slip. Sage and Coral's triplets were all adored by their parents, aunt, uncles, and grandparents, but Charity had always gravitated to Phoenix. Faith shared her Uncle Kip's love of animals, and Hope wanted to be a singer like Aunt Josie. Charity was already writing code and had recently helped Phoenix create a children's treasure hunting game. If the game was successful, the little girl's college education would be paid for before she finished grade school.

"To what do we owe this pleasure, Charity?"

"I only need sixty seconds of your time, Uncle Phoenix." Brandt's eyes went wide, but Phoenix kept his expression bland. If he gave her the slightest hint she'd surprised him, Charity would add a layer of drama, which always made it even more challenging to determine the real issue. When he nodded, she stiffened her spine as though she was getting ready to speak to the masses. "Is your system sluggish?" *What the hell?* This time he couldn't hold back his shock as he glanced at Charity in surprise.

"There are specialists who can have it running at peak performance in no time. I wrote down the eight hundred number. You can make the call, and they'll have your system purring like a fine tuned you're peeing motor."

"You're peeing? Darlin', I think you mean European." Brandt's correction earned him one of Charity's famous death glares. That particular expression had been known to send her Dominant father into orbit.

"That's what I said, Uncle Brandt. Please try to keep up, dear." Phoenix lost it. Charity was definitely spending too much time with their mom, and Sage needed to keep her from watching late night infomercials. Phoenix was laughing so hard he had tears streaming down his cheeks, but the combination of arrogant former SEAL and precocious preschooler was too much. Damn, he loved his family.

PACING HIS OFFICE like a caged tiger wasn't getting Dick Merrett any closer to a solution. He needed to put an end to his obsession with Reagan Walsh once and for all. At this point, he wasn't even interested in keeping her for himself. He just wanted to fuck her out of his system and then shut her up—permanently. Turning to his computer, Merrett signed in to his personal travel account and booked a flight and rental car.

The foolish woman who'd called him trying to extort money would need to be dealt with as well. Listening to her try to bull shit her way around him was laughable. He'd spent his entire career working with inmates. There wasn't a story, excuse, or angle he hadn't heard. Becoming hardened was just part and parcel for someone in his position. He deserved respect, even if it was from some bimbo in Bum-fuck, Montana. He'd teach her a lesson in protocol and the error of forgetting the significance of the chain of command. She'd think twice before she pulled that shit again.

He'd spent the past few days learning everything he could about Kelsey Jones and the company she worked for. He'd even stumbled on to an article in a tech magazine that talked about the small freight company's efforts to upgrade their security system. The article was five years old, but he doubted the small carrier had done any further upgrades. Getting in wasn't even going to be a challenge. Leaning back in his chair, he looked out over the prison facility compound and smiled. Damn, he'd set that bitch Reagan up perfectly. The inmate who'd attacked her was still enjoying the special favors he'd garnered, and the local county attorney hadn't even bothered charging him since the guy was currently serving multiple life sentences. *There's nobody more dangerous than someone with nothing to lose.*

Major Merrett tapped out a quick message to the Warden, letting him know he'd be gone for a few days on personal business. His boss responded immediately, assuring Merrett he'd cover his ass with H.R. That suited the shit out of Dick since his bitch ex was the Director of Human Resources. She'd have made him fill out a mountain of paperwork and asked him a hundred and one fucking questions—none of which he wanted to answer.

Driving home, he rolled down the windows of his truck to enjoy the cooler temperatures. Late fall in Texas probably meant it would be colder than a witch's tit in Montana. He'd need to pack some warm clothes—but nothing too bulky. After all, he had a sub to fuck. None of the submissives he'd scened with at his club in Dallas had been able to take his mind off Reagan. He'd known she was a sub the first time he'd met her, but she'd turned him down at every turn. Yea, that shit was about to come to a screeching halt.

Chapter Thirteen

RAFE PACED IN front of the wall of windows in his office. He'd had the floor to ceiling windows installed before he'd even moved in. The house was nice, but the one he planned to build would be show-stopping. Shaking his head and trying to push those reflections aside, he thought about the woman he'd left sleeping in his bed an hour ago. He'd slept through the night for the first time in years. It had been easy to tell how uneasy she was at first, but she'd relaxed into his embrace within minutes. Once she'd fallen asleep, she'd wiggled and squirmed until she was facing him, her entire body plastered against his.

Reagan Walsh was temptation personified. Her long chestnut colored hair flowed over his hands, and he'd threaded his fingers in the silky strands, ensuring she didn't move from his side without him knowing. She'd tucked her head under his chin so that her full breasts pressed against his abdomen, each breath she took intensifying the contact. Christ in heaven, Rafe had nearly come undone when she'd shifted against him, pushing her peaked nipples against him time and again. He'd recognized the rhythmic thrusts as an erotic dream immediately, but when she'd cried out his name, he'd fought the urge to roll her over and bury himself balls deep in her hot little pussy.

After watching her for weeks at the club, Rafe had been

stunned when another Dom remarked that Reagan was the least submissive waitress he'd ever seen working in a kink club. Rafe disagreed, but he hadn't responded—there wasn't any reason to tell the other man what he saw. *Why give the competition a heads-up?* Van Gibbs might be one of the club's Dungeon Monitors, but he was also a Master looking for a sub of his own.

Rafe was more pleased than he probably should be about last night's development. He'd suspected Reagan would submit to him because the desire always burned in her eyes. Her facial expressions softened any time he spoke to her, and he loved watching her pupils chase the chocolate brown of her eyes into narrow rings as they dilated with unspoken need. Hearing her whisper his name as she pressed her naked flesh against his had sealed her fate—even if she didn't know it yet.

He wondered if she would be disappointed to learn he had to return to San Francisco in a couple of hours. The call he'd gotten a few minutes ago from a friend he'd known since his undergraduate days had changed his plans. "You look deep in thought. Is it all right if I come in?" Reagan's quiet voice startled him, and he turned to see her standing in the open doorway. She'd put on the button-down shirt he'd been wearing yesterday, but she hadn't bothered to button it.

He didn't answer, just held out his hand to her. Without hesitation, she walked toward him, her bare feet completely silent as she crossed the carpeted room.

"You look beautiful, Peach. All sleep tousled and flushed with awareness and arousal. I'm glad you didn't button the shirt."

"I didn't know if I was supposed to dress. But when I came down the stairs, I thought I heard you talking to someone, so I wasn't sure you were alone." The worry in her voice made him feel like a heel. He should have gone up to check on her earlier.

"Since we haven't had a chance to go over our expectations yet, I'm counting this as a pleasant surprise." And he was, but it was also making it damned hard to tell her he had to leave. Taking her hand, he led her behind his desk. He sat in the large leather office chair and pulled her on to his lap. "I got a call from an old friend. His daughter was in an accident early this morning. She's sixteen and currently in surgery getting her leg pieced back together."

"Oh heavens. You have to go, don't you? I hope my oversleeping didn't delay you. Shoot, I hope she'll be okay." Such a soft heart. He hadn't even gotten a chance to tell her he felt bad about returning so much earlier than they'd planned. Reagan tried to stand, but he pulled her back down.

"Stay where I put you, Peach. You're not ready for the paddling you'd ordinarily get for that stunt." She went completely still, but he could feel the heat of her pussy against his denim clad thighs. Tapping the inside of her bare leg with his fingers. "Open for me. We'll use the same rules about being open to my touch no matter where we are."

"But, but I can't always have my pink bits exposed to the breeze. Holy shit, the local church guild will string me up. They won't care how many goodies I buy at their bake sales."

Rafe finally put his fingers over her lips to stem the torrent of words he was sure would continue flowing over them. Shaking his head, he chuckled before giving her a quick kiss. "Remember, you've given me dominion over those lovely pink bits, not the local bake sale brigade. It's my job to worry about when and where the fragrant rose petals of your sex are displayed." Reagan flushed the brightest scarlet he'd ever seen on a brunette, making him laugh, and he brushed the backs of his fingers over the heated flesh.

"Your safety and well-being are my number one priority, Peach. That's one of the reasons I hate the fact I have to leave so soon. Landon is going to drive me to the airport, so you'll have access to the SUV, but remember, you aren't allowed to drive until Ryan or Tally gives you the all clear. He'll be coming down in a couple of days to see you if she doesn't sign off before then." Rafe had spent the better part of two hours making calls, setting things in motion to move appointments in his clinic so he could return to Montana sooner and making sure Reagan would have plenty of people to rely on until she could drive. Tally had promised to check on her, as her friend and as a physician. Considering how tight their circle of friends at the club was, he wondered now if she'd get any rest.

"I've programmed Phoenix Morgan's phone number into your phone. Let him know if you leave the house. He'll also expect you to notify him anytime you open one of the doors. He's going to manage the security system from his end until we can get your biometrics entered into the system. I'd planned to drive you up there before I had to leave, but this will have to do in the interim."

"Oh wow. What happens if I forget? I don't want to cause him any trouble...or get myself into trouble."

Rafe was sure she hadn't intended to say the last part aloud, and he decided to let it go. "Reagan, I assure you, Phoenix is not going to be angry if you make a mistake. He runs a very successful security company, among other things. He knows how easy it is to forget to make the calls. If you don't call and he knows a door has been opened, he's going to call you." She sagged with relief and nodded. "Now, that being said...not answering your phone when he calls is going to bring the Calvary, so keep that in mind."

"Oh, brother."

An hour later, Rafe was packed and ready to walk out the door. Pulling Reagan into his arms, he sighed, "Baby, this is not how I saw the next few days playing out. I'm sorry."

"Well, if I hadn't gotten sliced and diced, we'd have had all the days I spent in the hospital. So there are two ways to view it." Her eyes were glassy with unshed tears, and he pulled her closer, pressing her against his chest.

"I've got to go. My ride is here, and I've scheduled things too tight to start out behind. Lock up behind me and keep your phone charged and on you at all times. I'll be back as soon as I can. Don't forget your meds, and you need to rest. I left you a meal in the microwave; make sure you eat it." He'd also left a note with her lunch and hoped it would give her something else to think about until one of their friends stopped by.

One scorching kiss later, he was on the other side of the door. He heard her engage the locks, but he also heard a soft sob. Walking away was one of the hardest things he'd ever done. How the hell did the men and women of the Prairie Winds Team do it? How did they leave their loved ones not knowing if they'd ever see them again? It also gave him a renewed appreciation for the men and women of the armed forces. He was only going to be gone for a few days, and it was killing him. *Suck it up, man. She isn't even yours...yet.*

"Sure, she is. But I'll let the two of you figure that out. Talking to yourself is one of the first signs you've fallen, by the way." Landon slapped him on the back and then climbed into this oversized truck. "Come on, let's go. I've got a naked woman to get home to, and you need to go do your hero plastic surgeon thing."

Great. Just fucking great. Landon was going home to his naked sub and Rafe was headed to an operating room where he would try to give a young woman her career back.

REAGAN WATCHED LANDON Nixon's truck disappear down the deserted street and turned back to the empty room. Wiping away her tears, she pulled in a deep breath. "Boy, this place seems a lot bigger now." She wasn't hungry, but Rafe had made such a point of telling her to eat she made her way to the kitchen.

"This kitchen is unbelievable. I swear he could host one of those Food Network shows in here." She saw a folded piece of paper with her name on it lying in the center of the breakfast bar, but before she could pick it up, her phone rang. The jarring noise in the quiet room startled her, and she dropped the phone, sending it skittering across the floor. "Dammit, I'm a fucking klutz."

When she finally wrapped her fingers around the slippery device, Reagan saw Phoenix Morgan's name on the caller ID. Answering, she could hear him chuckling. "Sweetie, you're going to give Calamity a run for her money, aren't you?"

"Pardon? Who's Calamity?"

"Kip's wife, Caila. Calamity is a nickname we tagged her with when she was a little girl. She's gotten better since she and Kip got married, but she is still an accident looking to happen when she gets flustered or she's distracted."

"Well, you just described me to perfectly...dammit."

"I'd say I'm sorry, but I'm not. And I didn't call to gossip about my family."

"Okay. Then to what do I owe this unexpected pleasure?" *Holy crap, this conversation just keeps getting weirder by the minute.*

"I wanted you to know I've turned on the inside cameras at Rafe's house as an added safety precaution for you." *Well, that explains why he compared me to his klutzy sister-in-law.* Her eyes darted around the room, but she didn't see any cameras. "Sweetie, you aren't going to see them. That's the point of having a security system. With Rafe out of town so much, we want to catch the bad guys. And we don't want them to know we're coming."

She had to admit what he said made sense. But it gave her the creeps to think about being watched 24/7. "Are there cameras in every room?"

"Yes. But I have not turned on the ones in the master bath. I am leaving those in the bedroom on simply because I want to know you are safe. I wanted you to know so you can have privacy and dress in the bathroom." *Why would he think I might not be safe?* "Listen, I can see that you're confused, but I'd appreciate it if you would humor me. I just spoke with Rafe a few minutes ago, and he asked me to turn the cameras on. He's not going to be able to call you for a few hours, but I promise he's got your best interests at heart."

"Ummm, okay. But I have to admit, I'm starting to worry."

"It's just a precaution. With Rafe leaving you sooner than he'd planned and your recent job change, he didn't feel comfortable leaving you alone in unfamiliar surroundings." Reagan might not be one of the all-knowing, all-seeing Doms from the Mountain Mastery Club, but she was no longer the naïve woman who'd thought she could save the world by volunteering at the prison, either. She recognized a snow-job when she heard one, and Phoenix Morgan had just sent a blizzard her way. Something was going on...she was sure of it; she just didn't know what.

Reagan had experienced this same underlying suspicion at the prison...she'd compared it to feeling as if she'd walked into the room during the middle of someone's story. Never being treated like one of the group. She'd been right, too. Once she turned down the advances of the newly divorced Major, she'd been shunned by her coworkers to the point she'd already contacted the volunteer organizer and given her notice. It was one thing to suck it up and ride out the tough times, but another matter entirely to stay where she no longer felt safe.

"What are you thinking, Reagan? Christ, you just went white as a fucking sheet." His voice startled her back to the moment, and she wondered how long she'd been lost in thought. "Reagan, if you don't start talking, I'm going to have people at the door in under five minutes. And I promise you, the people I send won't leave until they are convinced you're all right."

It might have been an exaggerated threat, but she didn't think so. Reagan had heard a lot about Phoenix Morgan, and the one thing everyone mentioned was his focus and attention to detail. *Fooling a Dom who's also a fucking Mensa isn't something I'm up to.* The room started to spin just as Phoenix's voice boomed all around her. "Sit down. NOW!" Somewhere in the back of her mind, she realized the sound hadn't come from her phone because it wasn't in her hand. *Speakers? There are speakers, too? It's just like being back in the facility. Eyes and ears everywhere. But will they help or hinder?*

Reagan perched on one of the bar stools. When she tried to put her head between her knees, she almost took a header off the damned thing. "Christ. What's taking them so long?" Just as Phoenix stopped speaking, she heard what sounded like squealing tires. Seconds later, the locks disengaged, and the door flew open. She was surrounded by people, but the voices began to blend together until she was back in the prison infirmary, surrounded by staff who'd ignored her cries for help. They'd only come to her rescue when several inmates she'd work with threatened to storm the small clinic themselves.

The noise in her head drowned out everything around her, and all Reagan wanted to do was make the cuts stop bleeding. There was so much blood. It flowed through her fingers even though she pressed them against her ribs until they ached. *Why isn't anyone worried about all the blood? There's so much blood. It's everywhere, and they act like they can't even see it.*

TAZ WAS THE first one through the door and almost stumbled when he hit the wall of emotion surrounding Reagan. She was having a flashback, and the terror was agonizing. Fuck, even he was fighting to remember it wasn't real. As an empath, Taz often dealt with strong emotions surrounding him. He could feel the emotions of most people if he allowed it, and he could actually hear the thoughts of an increasing number of people as his gift became more refined. But he'd never tried to reach out to anyone but his brother and wife.

Reagan, stop. There isn't any blood, sweetie. You're lost in a bad memory. Come back and let Tally check you over. He didn't get anything back but wild panic, so he tried again. *Your*

Master sent us to help you, Reagan. You told him you want to learn about the lifestyle. That means you listen to us when he's gone. Now look at me and only at me.

He'd felt the connection even before her eyes locked on his. Their souls connected for a split second, but it had been long enough for her to recognize him. Taz and Nate's grandmother was renowned healer, and she'd often described the moment when two souls touched one another. She'd insisted it could happen outside of love. Until that moment, Taz hadn't believed it was possible, but he recognized it the instant it happened.

Master Taz? How? Why are you here? Who are these people? Where is Rafe? He'd be able to see the blood, but he's not here. I'm really confused. The voice said sit down, and I did. But, but that wasn't good. I was too high. Why are the chairs so high? And no one is wearing uniforms now.

Taz could tell she was coming back, and he wanted to make the transition as easy as possible. He'd seen soldiers go from one flashback to the next if their minds weren't allowed to work at their own pace. She blinked her eyes trying to bring her surroundings into focus and blushed a brilliant shade of crimson Rafe would probably enjoy seeing as often as possible. Taz was standing to the side, but used his fingers to bring her attention to him. "Welcome back, sweetness. Have you had flashbacks before?"

"No. I had nightmares for a while, but even those faded quickly."

"Any idea what triggered it? What's the last thing you remember?" Taz listened as her mind flipped back though the pictures in her memory, recalling every detail of the time since Rafe left. He smiled when she zeroed in on the moment things changed.

"It isn't the security system really…and not that Phoenix can see and hear me. It's just that...well, I entrusted my safety to people monitoring cameras once. And as you know, it didn't end well."

He chuckled and nodded. "I'd say that's a fair statement. Now, let's get you settled in the living room so Tally can fuss over you for a few minutes before Koi whisks her away." Taz hadn't been surprised to see his brother-in-law and Tally drive in together. They were spending one on one time outside the club to find out if he was a good fit as their third. Taz didn't doubt the man would be able to hold his own during a scene. He'd known Koi for several years and had watched him scene with subs. SEALs in the lifestyle were a relatively small group and were well known to one another.

Tally stepped forward and buttoned the shirt Reagan wore, sending another flush over her pale cheeks. "Don't worry about it, girlfriend. You're in a room full of kinksters. This is business as usual for them. They'd have been more surprised to find you fully dressed moments after your Master left." Taz heard the denial that Rafe was *hers* bounce around inside her head, but a small spark of hope kept her from speaking up. *Good, that will keep her from saying something she'll feel bad about later.*

Moving to Rafe's office, Taz pulled out his phone and dialed Phoenix's number. He shared the suspicions he'd heard rolling around in Reagan's mind. There had to be a reason for this level of security, and he wanted to know what it was.

Chapter Fourteen

KOI WATCHED TALLY subtly check Reagan's pulse. When she moved her hand to her friend's back in what appeared to be a gesture of support, she'd been monitoring her respiration rate. He wasn't sure Reagan had realized what was happening, since she was still reeling from her earlier flashback. He and Tally had been driving near Rafe Newell's home when they'd gotten the call from Phoenix Morgan. Koi had to give the man credit, his timing was impeccable—they'd only been a half mile away, and from what he'd heard, Taz had been even closer.

Leaning against the breakfast bar, he watched Taz pull his phone from his pocket as he disappeared into what looked like an office. Pulling out his own phone, Koi typed a quick message to Micah Drake at Prairie Winds asking for a quick run-down of the situation. He sent a similar message to Phoenix. The two men worked together, but he'd learned a long time ago that, even given the same intel, different people would have slightly different perspectives of the exact same problem. Those minute differences often held the key—that one small detail often meant the difference between success and failure of a mission.

Phoenix sent him the report he'd pulled together so far, but there wasn't much detail about the man everyone was certain had orchestrated the attack on Reagan. After reading the medical report, it was a fucking miracle she wasn't having flashbacks on a regular basis. The facility's documentation indicated Reagan had said very little to the first responders, but the sworn statements from the EMTs who'd treated her once she'd been wheeled to the outside secured perimeter were entirely different.

The female EMT told the investigator that Reagan clutched her hand pleading with her to keep the prison staff away. She'd been particularly terrified of the Chief of Security—the Major she'd previously reported for inappropriate sexual advances.

When his phone buzzed again with an incoming message, he was surprised to see Micah's message. *I've attached both official and unofficial reports, but I'd suggest you contact Kirk Evans or Brian Bennett. They are members of the club, and Reagan was working for them as a Physician's Assistant when she was attacked. They helped her move to Montana and put her in touch with contacts who helped her find a job.*

What had started out as mild curiosity about Tally's friend was quickly turning into a cause. Why hadn't this woman's testimony been taken seriously? If something like this had happened to his sister, Koi would have been homicidal. He thanked both men for their help and moved into the living room. It was obvious Reagan was exhausted, but he suspected she wouldn't rest until everyone left.

"Tally." Both women shifted their attention to him, but he kept his focus on the woman he'd planned to spend the afternoon getting to know. "Come. It's time to go. Reagan needs to rest, and she isn't going to do that with everyone hovering over her."

"But..." He cut her off with a look any trained sub would recognize. He'd given her a command, and he expected her obedience. He was stricter than Karl, but he suspected she'd blossom under his intensity. Senator Tyson would be returning to Washington D.C. in a few days, and he'd asked Koi to spend as much time as possible with Tally.

Koi wasn't sure why the other man seemed almost desperate to secure a third in their relationship. But, since he was still technically on medical leave, he had the time, and spending time with a brilliant and beautiful submissive woman was anything but a hardship. Koi's gut instinct told him Karl's upcoming trip to Columbia wasn't going to end well, and he wondered if Karl didn't have similar concerns.

Five minutes later, they were back in the car. He'd hired one of the Dungeon Monitors to drive them today since he wanted to focus his attention on Tally. Reed Hughes was new to the club, so Tally didn't know him well enough to feel comfortable, which suited Koi's purpose perfectly. The air outside was crisp, but not as cold as it would be in a few weeks. Montana winters were not for the faint of heart, and he'd teased his beach-loving sister about her decision to move to a landlocked state where she'd been forced to buy her first winter coat.

Tally shivered as they hurried toward the warm car. "I'm already missing summer, and winter really hasn't even started yet."

"Reed's got the car all nice and toasty for you, *ma poupée*." The car would be the perfect temperature for a naked submissive. As soon as they were on the road, Koi turned to Tally. "Your hesitance when I called you to my side has earned you ten with a riding crop, Tally. But I'm going to give you the chance to reduce the number."

Her eyes widened, and he was pleased to see her expression fill with interest as well as desire. "I want to feel your lips wrapped around my cock, *ma poupée*. You have fifteen minutes to make me come. Every minute under that time limit removes one stroke of the crop." Tally's eyes were bright; the lady obviously loved a challenge. Koi leaned forward and rubbed his nose against hers. "Competitive, are you?"

"You have no idea." Her quietly muttered words amused him, but she was wrong. He knew a lot about the woman casting furtive looks at his rapidly inflating cock. The damned unruly appendage was pressing painfully against the zipper of his slacks, and he was anxious to free it from its confines.

"Strip. I want to see every inch of you while you take me to the back of your throat." It was nothing but the truth. The woman was a treasure, and Koi found himself wondering what the hell her husband was thinking leaving her alone clear across the country for weeks on end. There wasn't any doubt she was going to make him come long before the deadline. The intimacy of having his dick in her mouth, feeling her heat surround him, drawing him deeper was going to undo him quickly.

TALLY'S ENTIRE BODY hummed with desire. She'd seen Koi's reaction when she hadn't immediately moved to his side while there were still at Master Rafe's. Her hesitance hadn't been intentional, but she couldn't find it in her to regret the small slip. She'd been worried when Karl first introduced her to Koi. He'd seemed so aloof when they first met at Kodi's wedding she'd worried the three of them would never work together. She was much too spirited for a Dom who wasn't willing to engage. As a politician, Karl was every bit as outgoing as she was, perhaps more so; a Dom who held himself distant would never be a good fit.

To her surprise, Koi was turning out to be anything but emotionally distant. The connection between them grew stronger as they spent more time together. Tally hadn't realized how much she'd missed what a third brought into her life after Landon stepped aside. She was thrilled Landon had found a woman of his own and even happier that she and Savannah had become friends despite the odd dynamic of the situation.

Koi's command to strip sent a rush of moisture to her sex, and she felt her nipples draw up to tight points even though the car was toasty warm. When she let her gaze move to the front seat, Tally could have sworn she heard Koi growl. "Right now, I'm the only person you should be worrying about, *ma poupée*." The pet name made her smile. Ordinarily she'd balk at being called a doll. But since she'd never heard anything but affection in his voice, the pretty French endearment didn't sound condescending.

"Yes, Sir." The lines between his brows smoothed out at her response, and his entire body seemed to relax.

"I assure you, Master Reed will appreciate the view, because it's truly spectacular." Tally felt herself blush as she shimmied out of her jeans. "And I do appreciate the fact you aren't wearing panties, baby. When we get you started wearing dresses, all will be well." Most Masters wanted their subs to wear dresses or skirts when they were out in public together, but Karl had never cared that much. The only time he wanted unfettered access was when they were at the club. She could only imagine the fuss those in his D.C. social circle would put up if he slid his hand under the hem of her dress during one of their torturously long dinner parties.

"What are you thinking about, *ma poupée*? What put that light of devilment in your eyes?" Koi cupped his hand along the side of her face, focusing her attention on him. She'd gotten to know him a little, but she was worried he might not look kindly on her distraction...even if it had been amusing.

Never one to shy away from the truth, Tally answered honestly, explaining how much she hated the phony, uptight people Karl was forced to deal with as part of his position as a U.S. Senator. "I'm more than happy to stay right here and leave him to it." A cloud passed in Koi's eyes so quickly she wondered if she'd imagined it when she'd mentioned being perfectly happy to stay in Montana. She wasn't sure what that meant, but with her body vibrating in anticipation, she pushed the worry aside. A part of her knew what was coming, but she was going to remain in denial as long as possible.

Tally wasn't sure when he'd freed himself from behind his straining zipper, but when her hand brushed against the wet tip, her eyes fell immediately to his lap. His cock was long and thick, the veins roping their way up and around the length. When she unconsciously licked her lips, his laughter filled the large car. "*Ma poupée*, I don't know which side of you I enjoy the most—the playful side who finds amusement in the stuffed shirts in Washington or the vixen who is looking at my cock like she can't wait to feel it sliding over her tongue."

Since she didn't know what to say, she decided to not say anything at all. Both descriptions were accurate and there was another side of her he hadn't seen yet. When she was in full doctor-mode, she could be a force of nature. Most people underestimated her because of her size, but they learned quickly she could—and would—steamroll them without a moment's hesitation if they interfered with her patients' care. Her co-workers would never believe she was sexually submissive to one man, let alone two.

"Your time starts now, Tally." His words startled her back from her mental road trip, but it took her several seconds to make sense of what he said. When her eyes finally focused on him again, Koi was grinning and tapping the watch he wore on his left wrist. *Good God Gertie, who wears a watch now days? I wonder if all super spies wear them?* "Wear what? Do you know when you're speaking out loud? And just for the record, you're using up valuable time."

Tally ignored his questions, hoping they'd been rhetorical and leaned forward to caress the smooth head with the flat of her tongue. Encircling it with slow, wet strokes she savored his unique flavor and scent. He tasted like heated spices and smelled like an early summer morning in a rain forest. She continued licking until she made her way to the base and sent up a silent prayer of gratitude that Koi kept himself well-groomed.

The bulging veins pulsed against her lips, and his cock jerked when she sucked him deep. She pressed the top several inches of his rock-hard length against the roof of her mouth and heard him moan in response. When she looked up, his head was pressed against the back of the seat, but his eyes focused on her. The heat of his gaze had her redoubling her efforts. This wasn't about avoiding the punishment…she wanted to show him she would be worth the effort.

Tally always tried to be as honest with herself, and she was with others. Karl called her spirited, but that was just a very polite way to say she was a handful. Since she didn't have any plans to change, the only way to compensate was to be skilled when it came to sex. The only woman she'd ever met who'd instantly understood her logic was Tobi West. The two of them became fast friends when she and Gracie were helping set up the forum shops at Mountain Mastery.

Tobi had agreed wholeheartedly, while Gracie had insisted she saw her role with her Masters differently. Tobi had shaken her head and scoffed at her friend, "That's because you are a master of disguise, Gracie. You have your Masters convinced you are this sweet Latin American angel. How two men as smart as they are can't see through the sham is a mystery to me."

Gracie had howled with laughter and accused her best friend and business partner of being a green-eyed monster. Tobi had just grinned, "Yeah, yeah, yeah. Bite me, Barbarino." Tally's Spanish wasn't the best, but even she'd known Tobi's attempt to make Barbie sound Latin American had fallen short.

In the end, Tobi had looked at her and grinned. "For what it's worth, I agree completely. I'm not the best submissive...not by a long shot. And my Masters own a damned kink club for heaven's sake. I freely admit I'm not their best advertisement as BDSM Masters. But I work really hard at being worth all their effort." And that was what Tally was doing now. She was making all the work Koi was putting in getting to know her worth it. *Now, if he'll only keep me apprised of the time, I'll run out the clock. Then I'll get to make him come and still get my swats.*

KOI WAS FIGHTING what felt like a losing battle to keep his

eyes from popping out of his head. The pleasure robbed him of the ability to speak long enough for Tally to get the upper hand, and damed if the little minx didn't know exactly what effect she was having on him. The excitement in her eyes made her look even younger than she was. He'd been astonished to learn how much Tally had accomplished at such a young age. *She's no slouch when it comes to giving head, either.*

Koi tried to remember he was supposed to be the one in charge, hoping to pull himself back from the edge. He didn't want to come within the first two minutes. Hell, he'd planned to hold off until she still got the majority of the strokes. He'd been told she was a bit of a masochgist, and he'd wanted to ensure she got what she needed—even it it fucking killed him.

For the first time since he'd first been approached about becoming Karl and Tally's third, Koi worried he'd made a mistake. He'd known others who filled similar functions, and it seemed simple enough. Show up, help the Masteer fuck his sub until she doesn't know her own name, and then walk away with his heart and soul unscathed. But that was before he got to know Tally. Now he was worried she might very well steal his heart and soul if he wasn't careful. But fuck it all—how was he supposed to exercise any kind of caution when his brain was about to burst from pleasure?

Looking at his watch, Koi was amazed to discover he'd endured several minutes of her wet, velvet torture. Feeling her tongue lovingly caress the sensitive spot below the head was going to send him into orbit if he didn't wrest control back her. Threading his fingers through her hair, Koi let his palms cover her ears. Stilling her movements brought her eyes to his, and he could see the unspoken question in them. "No, you didn't do anything wrong. But you need to remember who is in charge."

Guiding her in a much slower pace than her nearly frantic stokes she'd worked herself up to, Koi watched his length disappear between her lips. Seeing her saliva shimmer over his skin as he withdrew had him lifting his hips in time with his hands guiding her down on to his cock. He felt the tip pressing against the back of her throat and moaned as white hot flashes of fire shot up the length of his spine. The vibration of her deep groan as she swallowed around him tipped the scales, and he let the release he'd been holding back sweep over him. Hot spurts of seed pulsed down her throat, and Tally took everything he gave her. He watched her shudder and relished knowing the little fox had just come without permission. The realization fueled his quick recovery, and he didn't waste any time setting his clothing right.

Koi effortlessly lifted Tally from the floor and flipped her over his knees before she had a moment to protest. Pushing two fingers into her soaking heat, he leaned down and nipped her shoulder. "You came without permission didn't you, *ma poupée*? Your pussy is drenched with your cream, the walls still quivering with aftershocks."

"Yes. I couldn't hold it back. Watching you…seeing the pleasure I could give you…mine streamed from yours. It was too much." Christ, her response was so perfect there was no way he could punish her for stealing an orgasm. Rotating his fingers, Koi pressed the tips against the spongy spot guaranteed to push her right back to the edge.

When a fresh wash of her arousal coated his fingers, he pulled them out and licked them clean. "You taste as sweet as you smell, pet. I'm going to give you the strokes you earned earlier. You do not have permission to come." He took the riding crop Reed was holding out for him and gave her a stinging slap, letting the leather flap snap against her bare flesh. She yelped, but he suspected it was more in surprise than genuine pain. When the imprint of the flap bloomed crimson, Koi knew he'd used the right amount of force. She was going to feel his marks for several days—and he suspected that was exactly what she wanted.

The next several strokes landed in quick succession, but never in the same place twice. By the time they were down to two, she was squirming on his lap trying to stall the orgasm he knew she'd been so close to. She had to feel his growing erection pressing against her side—the little troublemaker was going to make him come in his pants like an out of control teenager if he didn't get this wrapped up quickly.

"The last two are going to hurt, *ma poupée*, but you'll take them because they belong to you. You've earned them, but you've also earned the reward at the end. As soon as the second strike lands, you may come." He didn't give her time to tense up. The strokes were harsh, but lightning fast. Her body was already rocketing to release before her brain could process the pain. He dropped the crop and plunged his fingers deep into her pulsing channel just as a rush of her cream poured from between her swollen labia. Her scent filled the car, and Koi grinned when he heard Reed groan in the front seat.

Leaning down, he pressed a kiss against her shoulder. "You did so well, *ma poupée*. Rest for a moment and then we'll continue with our day. I want to spend the day exploring the area, and I think you'll be an excellent tour guide." She nodded, but he wasn't sure she was cognizant enough yet to respond, so he let the non-verbal response go.

He wondered if Karl had any clue what a lucky bastard he was. Tally was a treasure and deserved more than the short bursts of attention her husband gave her when he was home. And what was going to happen when Karl demanded she move to D.C.? Tally wasn't going to be happy living in a quagmire filled with backstabbing and deceit. Maybe he'd talk to Karl when he returned from his fact-finding trip; by then, Koi would have a better grasp on the subtle nuances of their marriage.

Pushing everything else aside, Koi focused his attention on the woman who still lay draped over his lap. He pulled a bottle of arnica gel from the small toy bag he'd tucked beneath the seat. Rubbing the soothing liquid over her ass cheeks felt as intimate as the punishment he'd meted out. "That's it, *ma poupée*. Let me take care of you. And then I have something special for you to wear while we take in some of the local sights." Yes, something *special* indeed. Reaching back into his bad, he retrieved the roll of PVC tape. He helped her sit up and watched her eyes widen when she saw the tape. Everything about her was an absolute delight, and he couldn't wait to wrap her up like the gift she was.

Chapter Fifteen

FOURTEEN HOURS AFTER he'd started, Rafe walked down the hospital corridor to speak with Keri's parents. The young woman's facial trauma had been more extensive than he'd anticipated, but everything had gone perfectly. If she followed his instructions, what little scarring remained would be easily concealed by make-up. After a short conversation with her very relieved family, he went in search of coffee.

Rafe turned on his phone and watched the screen fill with missed calls, voice mail notifications, and messages from everyone but Reagan. Why hadn't she texted? He'd left very detailed instructions in a note on the kitchen counter. But his frustration was quickly replaced by panic as the realization that something was wrong washed over him. What had happened that kept her from doing as he'd asked? That had to be the reason for all the messages and calls.

Moving quickly to one of the hospital's outside terraces so he'd have better phone reception and a bit of privacy, Koi began playing the voice mail messages. After the third call, he was no longer worried about Reagan's physical safety, but he was concerned about her emotional state. Rafe dialed Taz's number first in hopes he'd spent enough time with Reagan to give him the inside scoop. Taz's ability to connect with and read a person's emotions would make his insight invaluable in this instance.

When his friend answered on the first ring, he didn't waste any time with preliminaries. "I've been expecting your call. Have you gotten any sleep?"

"No. Talk to me." The coffee was finally kicking in, but the caffeine wasn't doing a thing for his patience.

"Reagan had a flashback. She said it was the first' and I believe her, although I think she could be misinterpreting some of what she calls 'lost moments'."

"Lost moments? What the hell does that mean?"

"She thinks of them as something akin to a daydream. But I've made a couple of calls, and the experts I spoke with agree that she's likely been experiencing mini-flashbacks and not recognizing what they were." Rafe leaned back into the chair and fought the urge to groan. Medical professionals were notorious for self-diagnosing—and their lack of perspective often led to inaccurate observations and decisions. Unfortunately, it was something they all were guilty of at one point or another.

"Have you spoken to her about this?" Rafe was curious whether or not she understood the significance of what she was going through.

"Not yet. I was waiting to talk to you. I know you don't have any real claim on her, yet, but I'm not sure you see it that way." Taz was right—on both points. Rafe had no idea why she'd become such an obsession. Hell, there were a lot of people who would consider it creepy. In any other venue, the level of security he'd left in place for her would probably be considered stalking. Thank God, his fellow Doms understood where he was coming from.

"You're right, but I haven't gotten to spend enough time with her to know if she's on board. She agreed to try, but every time I think we're going to get enough time alone to explore our mutual attraction, something fucking goes wrong."

"I understand. Maybe I should call Nanna-son and have her cleanse your aura or whatever it is that she does waving that bundle of smoking sage around. That shit stinks when it's burning, I'm telling you. I'm pretty sure the good juju flees right on the heels of the bad, but you'll never convince her or my mother. They've already set off the smoke alarms in our living unit twice this week. Nate threatened to change the codes on the elevator if they filled the place with smoke again. Although, to be honest, I'm not sure what was causing Kodi to cough the most, the damned smoke or the steam coming out Nate's ears."

Rafe heard his friend chuckle before he added, "Do you think it's really possible for a man's head to rotate like that little girl in that old horror movie? Because I'm telling you, I thought for a few minutes it was going to happen. If Kodi hadn't calmed him down, I think it might have been a Kodak moment for the ages."

Rafe couldn't hold back his laughter. It was probably exactly what his friend had intended, and Rafe was grateful for the distraction. He hadn't realized how tense he'd been until his shoulders relaxed for the first time in hours. "I'm not that desperate...yet. But I'm not going to rule it out, either. Your grandmother is a charming woman, and I wouldn't hesitate to ask for her help if I thought it was warranted."

"Goddess, you're a bigger suck up where she is concerned than Nix, and I didn't think that was possible." Taz didn't fool him. Both he and Nate adored their grandmother. Rafe had met the elderly tribal healer some time ago and liked her on sight. In many ways, she reminded him of his own, though his was usually more subtle in her machinations. "Listen, I know your first instinct is to get back here, thinking you can manage the situation, because that's what I'd want to do. But she's resting, and we've got everything covered. She might well see it as a sign you don't think she'd capable of handling herself. And I know she's already worried you'll change your mind about training her because she's more trouble than she's worth."

Rafe heard himself growl in frustration followed by Taz's laughter. "I do believe my brother and Brandt explained in detail what they thought of her remark. Something along the lines of helping with a paddling she'd never forget."

"I could arrange to come home, but it wouldn't be easy. And I think you might be right about her reaction. She made it clear the betrayal by the people she'd trusted to keep her safe was, in many ways, worse than the attack itself. I can see where rushing home to control the situation might be seen negatively." And he did see it, but that didn't mean he was thrilled to be leaving her alone.

"You can monitor the cams remotely, right?"

"Yes, but it feels a little like spying, especially given the fact that was what triggered her flashback today." It didn't feel quite right, but that didn't mean he wasn't going to check on her when he could. But the more people "watching" her, the more difficult it was going to be to justify it.

Rafe's second call was to Phoenix Morgan. "You can't possibly monitor the cams twenty-four hours a day? It's not reasonable for me to expect that."

"Don't forget I've got a team helping me. Just because we aren't all in the same room doesn't mean we aren't working as a unit."

Fuck it. Rafe hadn't meant to offend him, but the fatigue was taking a toll. "Look, man, I'm sorry."

"Don't even go there, Rafe. I understand. I'd be asking the same questions, and I know you're running on fumes. Talk to your girl, and then get some rest. We'll watch over her until you get home. But there's one more thing before I let you go." The tone of Phoenix's voice had shifted enough to put Rafe on guard. Whatever the other man was about to say wasn't going to be good news.

"After I did Reagan's initial background check when she applied to Mountain Mastery, I tagged some of the principals in the case. Richard Merrett—the head of security at the facility and the man Reagan felt was behind the attack—bought a plane ticket a couple of hours ago."

The man was dancing around something, and Rafe was losing patience. "Spit it out, man. I'm too tired to play twenty questions."

"His final destination is Missoula. I'm trying to find out if he has family or friends in the area, but I haven't turned up anything yet."

"When is his flight?"

"Not for a couple of days. If I don't turn up anything, I'll let Brandt know." He paused for a minute, but Rafe was certain there was more, so he waited in silence. "This might not have anything to do with the Major's travel plans, but Kelsey Jones called Brandt's office several hours ago. I'll let him give you the details of the call, but Brandt's theory is she tried to sell Reagan's location and her plan backfired."

"I swear I'll destroy her if she sold Reagan out." There wouldn't be a place on the planet she could hide from him. He rarely used his family connections, but he'd call in every available resource to take Kelsey Jones down.

"It would be another huge betrayal, that's for sure.

Trust is already going to be a big hurdle for you." And wasn't that the fucking understatement of the week? "And I'm going to give you a bit of advice. Get your temper under control before you call Reagan. She'll probably misread the anger and think she's to blame." Rafe heard the other man chuckle, "And don't bother to deny that you're fucking pissed as hell. I can hear it in your voice."

"Yeah. Taz said the same thing."

Phoenix burst out laughing. "I'm sure he did, but he cheats. I heard it the old-fashioned way." There was no arguing with that logic.

DICK MERRETT WALKED through the airport intent on retrieving the luggage he'd been forced to check. His Department of Corrections ID was the only reason he'd been allowed to check the damned bag. The agent hadn't been thrilled with the weapons stash, but he'd finally done the paperwork. Dick would have fired the jerk for treating a higher-ranking officer like a common criminal. That was one of the things he liked about working inside prisons. He had a lot more latitude with his staff. Anybody who believed the good ole boys club wasn't alive and well hadn't ever worked in corrections.

Retrieving his luggage, he made his way down the short hall to car rentals. Rubbing the back of his neck, Dick couldn't shake the feeling he was being watched. He'd surreptitiously scanned the area, but everyone he saw seemed absorbed in their own miserable life. He chalked it up to working in a place where there were only a handful of places where he wasn't under surveillance. One of the first things he'd done when he'd taken the position as Major was to remove the cameras from his office suite. As it turned out, that move alone had saved his ass countless times. If Reagan Walsh decided to sue, she'd never find any tangible proof he'd met with her assailant. Having a record of their meeting would cost the State of Texas millions and decimate his career.

He hadn't given a second thought to the fact Reagan might file suit against him until he'd started hearing rumors about some fancy-assed lawyer in Dallas asking for her contact information. Why else would some city center legal eagle be trying to get in touch with her? He intended to make sure she never saw one red cent.

In less than twenty minutes, he was on his way. He'd never been particularly close to his aunt's youngest son, but having a cousin in Montana was a great excuse to visit the state. There was also the added benefit of having a free place to crash for a few days while he tracked Reagan down. Of course, if the bitch who'd called him gave up the information as quickly as he anticipated, he wouldn't be in town long at all.

BRANDT LOOKED OVER Phoenix's shoulder at a tablet screen filled with pictures from the various security cameras in and around the airport. "Good thing Trixie still works for the car rental agency."

"It's even better that she doesn't hold a grudge or she wouldn't have done jack shit for you."

"Hey, that was years ago, and I've apologized to her more than once." Leaving her high and dry at a party their senior year hadn't been one of Brandt's finer moments. But since she'd met her husband that same evening, he'd never felt terribly guilty.

"Well, it seems the tracker is working. Since the air freight company is already closed for the evening, I'm curious to see where he's headed. The only family I could find living in the area was one cousin who claims he hadn't heard from Merrett in years before he got a call a few days ago. To say he was surprised would be an understatement."

"What makes you think he won't tell Merrett you were asking questions?"

Phoenix laughed and shook his head. "Because he applied to Mountain Mastery about a month ago. And somehow, he got the impression I'm still working on his background check. Strangest thing, it's been done for over a week."

"I have no idea why people think you're the *compassionate* brother."

"The women in our family love me because I use my super powers to help them with their Neanderthal husbands." Phoenix's ability to ingratiate himself with the Morgan wives was quickly becoming legendary.

"You *suck up* more than that souped-up vacuum you talked Dad into putting in the pool." Brandt shook his head when Phoenix's eyes lit up like it always had when he unwrapped a new electronic gadget at Christmas. "Swear to God, I'm nominating your wife for sainthood." They watched the blinking dot move slowly across the map. "He's headed to the cousin's house."

"Looks like it. I'd say you're clear until morning, but we'll keep watching."

Brandt nodded and moved to the door before turning

back to his brother. "What's your gut telling you?" Brandt's instincts were almost screaming that Merrett was here to finish what was started in Texas. But he was also the first to admit he was a paranoid bastard, so he wanted to hear what his brother had to say.

A couple of years ago, Phoenix became interested in profiling. One of the members of his Mensa Focus Group was the Chief Profiler for the FBI. The two of them, along with Phoenix's wife, Aspen, were collaborating on an interactive computer game centered on reading the clues left at murder scenes to profile the killer. Brandt didn't doubt it would be as successful as all of his brother's other games had been. The trio stood to make millions for their effort. And the fact Phoenix had approached this venture with the same run to the roar commitment he devoted to everything gave him a unique perspective into Major Merrett's thinking.

"He's here for Reagan. He set up the attack in Texas, but for some reason, the inmate stalled too long and the attack was interrupted. From studying the attacker's profile, I'd say he stalled because he actually liked Reagan. But Merrett wants to see her punished for rebuking his interest in her. She not only turned him down, but she was proactive when he continued to stalk her. She'd made it clear she would follow through on her threat to have him arrested if he didn't stop pursuing her." Brandt agreed, but knew his brother wasn't finished, so he held his tongue.

"Merrett is an egotistical prick. Everyone who works for him hates him. They pretend to be his friend to protect their jobs. Those who are good at the charade never have to worry about being fired for infractions that send others out the door. He likes nothing better than to humiliate and shame those who cross him. He couldn't care less about public safety or rehabilitation and treats the inmate population like little more than dirt beneath his feet."

"And you think he's here to finish what he started?" So far, Brandt agreed with everything Phoenix said, but he appreciated the confirmation.

"No question about it. But I also think he'll want what she denied him." Brandt felt his eyes widen at the thought.

"I don't think he wants *her* as much as he doesn't want to be denied a prize he thinks he deserved." Phoenix appeared to be choosing his next words carefully, and that hesitance was unusual between them. "Listen, everything about this man is a half-bubble off-center. Be careful. And we need to make sure Rafe knows what he's up against." Brandt didn't respond. He simply nodded his understanding and stepped out into the hall.

He wasn't going to call Rafe until morning. The last time they'd spoken, the man was so exhausted he'd started rambling in the middle of their conversation. Brandt had been there too many times to count during his years in the military. It was a dangerous place where bad decisions looked perfectly reasonable and even the most patient men and women came apart at the seams with the slightest provocation. Rafe needed the sleep more than he needed the worry.

Chapter Sixteen

THE RINGING OF a phone pulled Reagan from the depths of sleep and straight up pissed her off. The fog surrounding her made it too difficult to see the offending device, and she wished a very painful death on whoever owned it. As soon as it stopped, she slid back into the peaceful darkness. The quiet was like a warm blanket wrapped around her, lulling her deeper into sleep. The bed she was lying on felt more like a fluffy cloud, and the sheets were silky soft brushing against her bare skin. Stretching her legs before curling around a pillow that smelled like the man from her dreams, Reagan drifted deeper into sleep when the ringing started once again.

I'm going to kick somebody's ass if they don't answer their fucking phone. The thought sailed through her mind a split second before what sounded like a shotgun blast against the wall beside her. Kicking her way free from the sheet tangled around her legs, Reagan lost her balance and hit the floor with a resounding thud. The pounding outside the bedroom stopped, but resumed a few seconds later closer to the front of the house. Vaulting to her feet, Reagan ran straight into the bedroom door, knocking her right back onto her ass. "Fuck a fat duck."

Getting back to her feet, she brushed the hair from her eyes and grabbed her glasses from the nightstand. Whoever was beating down the door wasn't going to wait while she brushed her teeth and put her contacts in, so they were just going to have to cope with her looking like a homeless person who'd just been kicked out of their box. "Shit, that would be funnier if it wasn't so close to the truth."

She was almost to the front door when she remembered her phone. Taz and Nate had made her promise to keep it on her at all times, so she turned and sprinted back to the bedroom. Picking it up, she noted fourteen missed calls from Rafe and a couple from Brandt Morgan. "Why do I have the sheriff's phone number in my phone? Boy, I'll bet Rafe was worried." She pulled the door open without checking the peephole to face a scowling Brandt Morgan.

"Damn right, he's worried. And he's going to be pissed when he finds out you opened the door without checking to see who was on the other side." His glare almost singed her eyebrows it was so hot.

"Good morning to you, too, Sheriff. And how do you know I didn't check the peephole?"

"It's two o'clock in the afternoon, Reagan." *Well, la-te-fucking-da. So I overslept.* "It's two o'clock *Friday* afternoon. And you didn't have time to check."

"Friday? What the hell happened to Thursday?" She hadn't intended to ask the questions out loud, but she'd been so shocked they slipped out before she could filter them.

His gaze swept over her, but there wasn't any heat in it. "Go get dressed before the Calvary arrives. I'll put on some coffee, and hopefully, that will get that dazed look out of your eyes before your video call with Rafe." She was trying to keep up, but he was speaking too fast for her sleep fogged brain. *Dazed look? What does he expect? I just woke up.* "Move." His sharp command and the clap of his hands startled her into action.

"Hang on to your danglers, for Pete's sake...I'm going." She would have laughed at the mortified expression on his face if she hadn't worried it would be just one more strike against her, and she was already sinking like the Titanic. She heard his phone ring as she ran down the hall, but didn't stick around to find out who he was talking to. Stepping into Rafe's enormous master bath, she took one peek at her reflection in the mirror and screamed. Her hair was a tangle of wild curls sticking out every direction, reminding her of the cartoon characters she'd seen who'd been electrocuted. She was deathly pale. Her sun deprived skin was so light she'd probably glow in the dark. And there was a lot of skin showing since she was only wearing a skin-tight tank top that didn't reach her bikini panties.

The door of the bathroom sounded like it was being knocked off its hinges, making her jump across the room and slap a hand over her mouth to stifle another scream. "Are you all right?"

Sucking in a deep breath, she replied, "Yes. I just saw myself in the mirror."

She heard him chuckle before returning to whoever he'd been speaking to on the phone. "She's fine, just freaked out because her hair's messy." *Messy?* Holy shit, it looked like she'd combed it with an egg-beater.

Glancing down at the counter, Reagan noticed the pain pills Rafe left her were scattered over it. *Well, that explains the lost day.* She'd never been able to handle pain meds, and these were particularly potent because he'd known she was having trouble sleeping. Scooping them up and dropping them back into the bottle, she set it in a drawer, vowing to not touch them again. A chill ran up her spine when she thought about how vulnerable she'd been. Rafe's house had great security, so at least they'd have pictures of who broke in and murdered her in her sleep. Shaking her head at the dark humor, Reagan peeled off what little she was wearing and stepped into the massive shower.

As the hot water slid through her hair, Reagan admired the enclosure. The rock walls hid smaller shower heads at various heights, and she wondered how many times Rafe had used them to torture some poor sub. Thinking about him sharing this shower with another woman made her chest clench in something too close to jealousy for her comfort. It was ridiculous to feel possessive of a man she didn't have any real claim on. "Just because he's letting you stay in his house doesn't mean he belongs to you."

"Seems legit to me. You are sleeping in his bed. That probably means something." Kodi's voice sounded from the other said of the shower wall, making Reagan gasp in surprise.

"Well, personally, I always thought the rule was if you licked it, it was yours. Have you licked him yet, Reagan?" Tally's laughter bounced off the marble in the bathroom, sounding like she was closer than Reagan hoped she actually was.

"Please tell me you aren't in the bathroom." Reagan's question was muffled by the water falling all around her, but if the women were close, they wouldn't have any trouble hearing her.

"Okay…we're not in the bathroom." Tally's light-hearted tone gave away the fact she wasn't serious.

"Tally, you aren't supposed to lie." Kodi's mock exasperation with her friend made Reagan smile.

"Not my fault. She said to tell her we aren't in here…so I did. I'm like that, you know? All compliant and shit. Besides, she didn't ask me if we were here. If I said no, then, well, that would be lying." Dr. Tally Tyson could always make those around her smile. She'd been one of the first members to befriend Reagan when she started working at the club.

Reagan leaned her forehead against the smooth rock below the showerhead, closed her eyes, and sighed. "Dammit, I haven't been up long enough for this nonsense."

"Well, Tramadol will kick your ass if you aren't careful, sister." Reagan's gasp must have been loud enough for the other women to hear, because they both snickered.

"Dammit, I thought I put those away."

"You missed one on the floor, which tells me you don't even remember taking the second or third round." Reagan groaned in frustration. "And *this* is why I won't give this to my post-op patients unless I know they have someone at home to administer it. I'm guessing Rafe thought one of us or your medical background would help."

"I don't usually take opioids, because they kick my ass. But everything hurt before I went to bed. And no, I don't remember getting up or spilling the pills. That must be why I slept so long. And that's confidential information, by the way."

"Well, that covers me. I can claim HIPPA as a defense, but Kodi is screwed."

"Did I hear my name? Oh dear, I was looking at this lovely marble and not paying attention. I'm like that sometimes, off in my own little world...thinking about my next book."

"Jesus, Joseph, and sweet Mother Mary. We get it already. Save the drama for your readers. Hey, speaking of readers, when is your next book due? I'm dying to hear what happens with Gianna. That bitch makes my blood boil."

The two women moved out of the bathroom amid a lively discussion about whether or not Tally could claim friendship privileges and get the scoop on Kodi's upcoming release. Reagan was out of the shower and dressed in the clothing her friends had left on the counter in record time. She was grateful for their help since she'd forgotten to grab anything and certainly hadn't been looking forward to walking back into the bedroom wearing nothing but a towel knowing the room had cameras.

Deciding a braid was the quickest solution for the hair, Reagan was securing the bottom when Brandt stepped into the doorway. "Rafe is on a video call for you downstairs. Hop to. He's out of patience, and I don't blame him. You were just supposed to throw on some clothes." Shaking his head, he turned, and she heard him muttering something about women fighting wars naked because they'd never be ready on time as he stomped out of the room.

Tally giggled as Reagan walked by. Cupping the underside of her breasts, she lifted them as if offering them up for inspection. "Who's he kidding? If we show up for a war naked, it'll be the shortest conflict in history."

"Good grief." Kodi's admonishment earned her a negligent shrug. Reagan appreciated their antics. Now to get through the next few minutes without being put out on the street.

RAFE WAS ABOUT to give up on the video call and fly back to Montana when Reagan finally slid into view. "Peach, I've been so worried about you."

He saw her blanch before she ducked her head. "I'm sorry. I shouldn't have taken the pain killers. I know better. But everything hurt. And I just needed to sleep."

Fucking hell, he felt two inches tall. "Baby, I wasn't scolding you. I was just so relieved to see for myself you're all right. Don't take any more of the meds unless someone is there with you. I've been calling for hours, and Brandt was worried he wasn't going to be able to wake you without going inside." Her expression told him she understood how vulnerable she'd been.

"Do you want me to leave? I understand. I've been nothing but trouble. Geez, even Phoenix Morgan thinks I'm a trouble magnet like his sister."

"Sister-in-law, sweetness. And saying you are like Calamity is probably one of the nicest compliments he could have given you. We all love Caila." Rafe could tell Reagan hadn't even realized Brandt was standing in the room until he spoke. She gave Brandt a small smile in acknowledgement and then returned her attention to him.

"In answer to your question, no, I do not want you to leave. As a matter of fact, I don't want you leaving the house unless one of the Masters from the club is with you." He could see her surprise and planned to tread carefully. He wanted her to be alert, but not terrified. After his conversation with Brandt, he was worried she'd run if she discovered Merrett was in Montana. And finding out he was less than thirty minutes away could easily send her into another flashback or panic attack.

Her brown eyes were filled with apprehension, and not the kind a Dom enjoyed seeing, either. Taking a deep breath, he continued, "Dick Merrett is on vacation, sweetness."

"Vacation? Why would I care that he's on vacation?" If

he hadn't been watching her carefully, he might have missed the way her spine straightened and her shoulders tensed beneath the well-worn t-shirt she wore.

"He's in Montana, visiting family about a half-hour from Missoula. We have no reason to believe he knows where you are, but I'd prefer to err on the side of the angels." When she didn't respond, he tapped the screen and split his view so he could see Brandt. Much to Rafe's relief, his friend was still standing in the room, and he'd shifted his position so he had a better view of her facial expressions. The creases between the sheriff's brows weren't a good sign.

"Don't even think about running, baby." She jerked her gaze up to his, and Rafe barely restrained the curses burning on the tip of his tongue. Deliberately softening his expression and voice, he leaned fractionally closer to the screen and whispered, "You said you wanted to learn. We've been shut down twice, baby. My grandmother always told me the third time's a charm, and, sweetheart, I will be home in two days. We'll talk again about my arrival, but for now, I want you to promise me you won't leave the house without one of the Masters as an escort."

She was staring at him, but he wasn't sure she'd grasped everything he'd said. He didn't want to end the conversation until he was certain she was onboard, but he'd already been paged twice. If he had any prayer of returning to Montana on schedule, he needed to get back to work.

The third time his pager pinged, Reagan seemed to zero in on the sound. "That's your pager, isn't it? And it's not the first time it's gone off, so I know you need to go. I promise I won't leave the house. I'm sure there is plenty here for me to eat." She was right. There was plenty of food in the house, and the freezer was also fully stocked.

Hell, she could probably hole up there for months if she didn't need perishables.

"Look for the letter on the counter, baby. I left it there the day I left, but fate has a way of interfering in my best laid plans to get you under me." Or in the case of the note he'd left, naked and ready for the steamy video call he'd hoped to enjoy twenty-four hours ago. "Keep your phone on you, Peach. I'll be calling to chat again in a couple of hours. Tally will be supervising your medication, and I suspect she'll be making changes. Be a good girl and follow her directions."

"Okay." When he raised his brow and leveled a look at her that all subs recognized, she quickly amended her response. "Yes, Sir." After signing off, he sent a quick message to Tally asking her to prescribe something milder and to dispense it personally. He wasn't going to take any chances with Reagan's safety.

After ending the call, Rafe pushed back from the desk and paused. How had she become so important to him amid so much chaos? She'd captured his interest the first day he'd seen her at the airport, and everything about her brought his protective instincts roaring to the surface. Shaking his head, he got to his feet. It was time to get back to work. Thankfully, he'd shifted enough appointments around he should be busy enough that he might be able to forget the fact he still hadn't gotten to feel Reagan's body beneath his. But he was determined to give her the introduction to the lifestyle she wanted as soon as possible, and fate just needed to cooperate this time.

Chapter Seventeen

By noon the next day, Reagan was ready to crawl out of her skin. Why on Earth had she promised Rafe she wouldn't leave the house? Just the thought of being cooped up for another thirty-six hours made her want to jump off a bridge. In between Rafe's call and texts, she'd polished everything she could reach, including the three cars in his garage. *Why does one man need three cars?* She could understand having two. After all, it wasn't hard to imagine one being unavailable due to repairs or maintenance. But three? That seemed like overkill to her.

When she'd questioned him about his *fleet*, he'd laughed and informed her she hadn't seen the cars he kept in the shed behind the house or the ones in San Francisco. Her mouth dropped open, and he'd burst out laughing. When she'd scowled at him, he'd given her a heated stare. "Oh, baby, that glare just earned you time over my knees. Glaring at your Master is never a good idea."

Before she'd been able to pull the words back, she'd snipped, "You were laughing at me, and I didn't like it."

"I'd have thought you would be pleased because you'd given me something to smile about after a very difficult day." She hadn't thought of it that way, but it still didn't seem fair that she was going to be punished just because his ego couldn't tolerate a frown. "You're overthinking it,

Reagan. Did you read any of the material I forwarded to you?"

"Yes. I read it all…twice." And she had. She'd also done some on-line research of her own. Not that it had done her any good, because now she had more questions than answers.

"Questions?"

Yes, but none that I'm brave enough to ask you. How am supposed to ask you if it's true that some Masters give their submissives to other men to fuck? How do I tell you how much that idea terrifies me? How will I ever be able to explain how worried I am Brandt Morgan will follow through on his threat to help give me a paddling I'll never forget?

"Reagan." His sharp tone startled her out of her musing. Focusing on his face, she suddenly realized this was the perfect opportunity to ask those very questions. He wasn't here. He was several states away. If he got angry, she could leave before he returned, and she'd never have to face him and admit she was too frightened to really try.

"I don't know what's going through that sharp mind of yours, but I'm starting to appreciate Karl's dilemma with Tally. It seems very bright submissives present a whole new level of challenge." She couldn't hold back her smile, because being compared to Tally wasn't an insult. The doctor and Kodi had been checking on her so often, it was a wonder she'd had time to get cabin fever. "What are your questions, Peach?"

Taking a deep breath, Reagan let them all spill out without pause. When she'd finished, she gulped in a deep breath to banish the black dots dancing in her vision. This time Rafe's soft laughter made her smile. "Decided to spit it all out while I wasn't there, did you?"

Heat immediately infused her, and she was certain her

cheeks were flame red. Busted. "Yes, Sir." There was no reason to deny what was evidently perfectly obvious.

"First of all, remember I agreed to train you. That means I expect you to ask questions. I'd be more upset if you didn't, because I'd worry you weren't showing enough concern for your own well-being." Was he serious? He wanted her to ask questions? She hadn't done a lot of dating, but those few men had never invited questions. "As long as your questions are stated respectfully, I'll answer them. Until we know one another better, I'll expect you to talk to me about anything that concerns you, particularly anything that frightens you."

Relief washed over her, and she felt herself sag in the chair. His expression softened, but his dark eyes were as intense as she'd ever seen them. "The single most important part of the D/s lifestyle is communication. Until we are intimately familiar with each other's preferences and habits, we'll negotiate everything. That requires your honesty. I'll need to know that you'll tell me if something isn't working for you or if you're frightened."

"I don't want another Master to...well, I don't want them to have..."

"Sex with you? Is that what you were trying to say? That you don't want another Master to fuck you? Peach, the last thing I want to do is share you. Leaving you in their care these past few days has driven me to distraction." And the thought of sharing her pleasure with another man made his gut tighten. He'd never been the jealous type, but everything was different with Reagan.

"Nothing happens that you don't want to happen, baby. You have safe words for a reason." Her eyes filled with tears, but she fought to keep them from falling as she wrapped her arms around herself. As if he'd read her mind, his next words sent the tears spilling down her cheeks in a cascade of pain-filled loneliness. "I wish I was there to hold you, Peach. No one should ever underestimate the healing power of touch. A hug from someone who genuinely cares about your well-being is the best medicine in the world." Short of bursting into a full-blown crying jag, nodding was her only option. "You're breaking my heart, baby."

"I'm sorry…it's just that I'm not used to having so much free time. I haven't watched television in so long I don't even know where to start. And it's not fair for me to expect Kodi and Tally to be here all the time. And for some reason, Sheriff Morgan insisted I not contact Kelsey."

RAFE HAD HOPED to have this conversation in person rather than during a video call, but it would be wrong to not explain now that she'd mentioned Kelsey. "How much do you know about Kelsey outside of work, Reagan?" He suspected it was the use of her real name that made her sit up a bit straighter before she answered.

"Not much at all. We had drinks after work a couple of times, but it was always with a group so our conversations weren't private. I ate lunch with her a few times, but all she did was talk about a Master at the club she wanted to hook up with." She must have seen something in his expression that caught her attention, because she paused, leaning forward fractionally. "When I asked her about it several weeks later, she said she'd gone to the west coast to see him, but it didn't go well."

He took a deep breath and shook his head. "No, Peach. It didn't go well at all."

"It was you? You were the Master she was so convinced was her ticket out of what she called the drudgery of working? She must have been really amused when she figured out I…"

"When you what, Reagan?" Rafe was fairly certain what she'd been going to say, but he wanted to hear her say the words.

The crimson tinting her cheeks made him want to brush his fingers over them. It would be a joy to feel the heat of her embarrassment beneath his fingertips. "She always laughed at my interest in you. Her mocking attitude makes sense now. I feel pretty foolish for not putting it together."

"Don't. If there is one thing I've learned from my encounters with Kelsey, it's that she is very capable of masking her true self."

"Did you? No. Never mind, it's none of my business." She'd suddenly realized how personal her inquiry would have been, so she cut it off before she embarrassed herself.

"Reagan, I've already told you I expect you to ask questions. There will be times I won't answer, but I'll always explain why. If you were going to ask if I fucked her, then the answer is no. I did a couple of scenes with her at the club, but I'm not as fond of public sex as some of the other Masters. Scenes can be very intimate, but for me, they are more about pushing the sub's boundaries and helping them explore their sexuality. When I'm balls deep in your tight little pussy, I don't want you thinking about an audience."

Her face flamed again, and he wondered if she would always be embarrassed by the blunt language that was considered normal among club members. "I don't think I'd be comfortable having sex in front of a large group of people." Rafe didn't doubt her self-assessment was accurate. He'd read her club information, but he'd also asked Phoenix for a background check. Rafe's family connections made him cautious. His father's international tech company had made him a multi-millionaire before he was thirty. But it had been the elder Newell's marriage that cemented him as a force to be reckoned with on Wall Street. Rafe's mother was a member of one of Europe's oldest banking families.

Rafe had never been interested in either his dad's tech business or his maternal family's banking business. Remarkably, his parents had always encouraged both Rafe and his sister to pursue their own dreams. In many ways, he'd considered medicine a way to give back after having been given so much.

Reagan, on the other hand, had been born into a lower-middle class working family. She'd studied hard in order to get the scholarships she needed to attend college. Her parents were killed on their way to her college graduation when a drunk driver crossed the centerline hitting them head-on. Drs. Kirk Evans and Brian Bennett told Phoenix they'd been blown away when she shown up to work a week later.

The two gynecologists had recruited the newly minted Physician's Assistant during her final semester, but when they'd heard about the accident, they'd offered her a later starting date. She'd politely refused, hit the ground running, and had never missed a day of work until the attack at a nearby prison. She'd worked hard for everything she'd had and then lost it all because she'd turned down a power-hungry ass hat who refused to take no for an answer.

The scars from that attack, both physical and emotional, would likely make her reluctant to be completely vulnerable in front of an audience. Knowing the security staff at the prison watched the attack before interceding would make the most exhibitionistic submissive think twice before fucking in public.

Deciding it was time to lighten the mood, Rafe gave her a sly smile. "We'll discuss the details soon, Peach. But before we end this call, I have a surprise for you. Kodi and Tally will be arriving soon. Nate and Koi will be escorting the three of you to the spa at Mountain Mastery." He frowned when she started shaking her head.

"I'm sorry. I know you are trying to help me stay busy, but I don't have the money to spend on spa treatments. I'm sure they are really expensive…not that I'd actually know. But it seems like a reasonable assumption. Tally makes good money as a surgeon, and Kodi's books are selling like hot cakes. Unfortunately, waitresses don't make enough to have disposable income. But I really do…"

"Stop talking." His barked command garnered him glares from a couple of women walking down the corridor. It's a wonder Reagan hadn't fallen off her chair if he'd shouted loud enough to be heard through the glass wall of his office. "Baby, I've already made all the arrangements. It's a Master's privilege and duty to provide for his submissive. I assure you, neither Tally nor Kodi are paying for their own spa treatments. Their Masters have already chosen what treatments they'll have and paid for them. When I learn your preferences, I'll take those into account, but this time, I've made the selections."

Leaning closer to the screen, he gave her a smile guaranteed to make even the most inexperienced submissive shudder. "Remember, you only have two obligations at this point in your training—keeping yourself safe and pleasing your Master. It will please me very much to know you are having fun this afternoon at the spa with the ladies.

And I'll enjoy the fruits of this afternoon's visit when I return." When her cheeks flushed, he couldn't hold back his chuckle.

"Thank you. You're too kind." Her sweet voice reminded him just how new she was to the lifestyle. Most subs would know their Master had something up his sleeve, and Reagan would learn that lesson soon enough.

This time, he laughed out loud. "Oh, Peach, you might not think I'm so sweet later this afternoon. Since you'll have a designated driver, I encourage you to enjoy the drinks they'll be serving."

After they'd ended the call, Rafe didn't waste any time getting back to work. With a little bit of luck, he'd be back in Montana in time for dinner tomorrow evening. He sent up a silent prayer that fate didn't choose to ignore his grandmother's third time's a charm rule.

Chapter Eighteen

REAGAN WAS RELIEVED when they stepped inside the Mountain Mastery Spa. She'd been sandwiched between Koi and Nate during the short walk from the parking lot. The two of them dwarfed her, and the whole thing had been intimidating as hell. As soon as she was safely inside, the men quickly said their goodbyes and disappeared.

"Damn, girlfriend, you should feel like a rock star or royalty. That prick from Texas sure has the men all on alert." Leave it to Tally to break the tension by getting straight to the point.

"You have the finesse of a bull in a china closet, Tally. Didn't you have to take some classes in people skills or bedside manner or, hell, tact?" Kodi's laughter let them know she was teasing, and Tally was obviously unfazed because she'd given her friend the middle finger before returning her attention to Reagan.

"Don't mind her. You know how authors are? They'll smother you in flowery words, and by the time they actually get to the point, your head's rolling around on your shoulders and you're two shakes from dead asleep."

Reagan shook her head at their antics, but she had to admit that she'd found Nate and Koi's hovering unsettling. It made her wonder if they knew something she didn't.

Before she could fall into a funk, Kodi grabbed her hand and pulled her around the counter. "Come on! You have several appointments, so we can't waste any time. And besides, the sooner you start, the quicker they bring out the goodies."

"No happy juice for you, Kodi," Tally reminded.

Reagan had forgotten Rafe's casual remark on Kodi's pregnancy. With all that had happened, she'd forgotten to see if he'd been right. "So, you *are* pregnant?" When Kodi nodded, Reagan jumped up and down in a ridiculous happy dance that made both the other women giggle like school girls.

"Yes. Nate and Taz bought all the pregnancy tests at the drug store and made me do them all before we met their grandmother for dinner. They should have saved the money. She took one look at me and started grinning. Now that I think about it, she danced a jig just like the one you did."

"That's so exciting. I loved working at Kirk and Brian's gynecology clinic. It wasn't all sunshine and roses, but most of the ladies were thrilled to be bringing a new life into the world. Watching their faces light up when they talked about the baby's future was always the highlight of my day."

"See? There you go…a sounding board. You can ask Reagan all your questions. Your obstetrician will be thrilled, and I'm off the hook since that is *NOT* my specialty." Grabbing Reagan's hand, she pulled her through the curtain at the back of the small reception area where a woman dressed in yoga clothing stood smiling at the three of them. "Let's go. You and I get to celebrate with our beverages of choice. Kodi gets juice for her little *bambino*."

"Oh brother, please tell me I don't have to do yoga."

"Dr. Newell suggested we work on flexibility for a few minutes several times this afternoon, so you'll be seeing me frequently." The tiny woman looked like she was made of wire. There wasn't any way Reagan was going to be able to keep up with her on a yoga mat.

Kodi and Tally both burst out laughing when she felt her mouth drop open in shock. "Please tell me you are joking. Please? I'm the most uncoordinated person you know…unless I'm swimming. I'm actually pretty good at that."

Kodi nudged her and grinned. "Maybe you can talk Tabby the Torturer into water yoga. Then you can drown her and save the rest of us."

"Do not tell me that Master Koi signed me up for yoga." When the smiling woman nodded, Tally groaned. "Good Lord, military men are the worst. They think everyone should be in the same physical shape they're in. None of them seem to understand not all woman want to be able to wrap their ankles behind their heads and dance on their tippy-toes for their Master's entertainment."

"But flexibility will help Kodi give birth naturally, and it will help all of you enjoy your sexual encounters more." Tabby's enthusiasm was beginning to wear thin, and Kodi had gone white as a sheet.

"Crazy Lady Alert. Who said I wanted to do natural childbirth?" Looking frantically at Reagan, Kodi's voice went up a full octave. "You have to tell my husbands that an epidural isn't a sign of weakness. I don't want to hate them while our angel is coming into the world. And I will…you know I will. And I can be mean. You think my brother is wicked bossy…oh, you haven't seen anything yet. Just thinking about natural childbirth scares me to death."

Reagan giggled at the desperation in Kodi's voice. "You have a lot of time to convince them, but I'd be happy to explain the benefits of a reduced stress birth to them."

"Damn, that's great PC BS right there. I'm telling you it doesn't get any more sugar-coated than that. Politically correct bull-shit is a skill...and Reagan is obviously a pro. Kudos." Tally's deep bow made everyone around her laugh. Standing up, she shuddered before nodding into the room Tabby had disappeared in to. "Come on. Let's get this over with so we can get to the booze."

Twenty minutes later, Reagan lay sprawled on the mat panting. If she could just pull in a little more oxygen, maybe she'd be able to crawl out of the room. "Holy hell. Tabby the Torturer is the meanest woman I've ever met in my entire life." Turning her head to the side, she drilled Kodi with a glare. "And your husbands pay her to do this to you?" Kodi's nod was so slight it was almost imperceptible. "Mercy. And they seem like such nice men."

This time Kodi turned her head and glared. "Nice? Really? Wow. And here I thought you were bright." Tally snorted a laugh from Reagan's other side, but it would have taken too much effort to turn and give her a sweltering look.

"Come on, ladies. You're off to your respective estheticians." The chipper voice of the yoga beast grated on Reagan's nerves. *There ought to be law against perky torturers.*

Rolling to her feet, Reagan helped Kodi then stood close until she was sure the other woman was steady on her feet. "Thanks. Sometimes I stand up too quickly, and everything swirls around me."

"Remember, you're sharing your blood supply now, but that's something you'll need to mention to your doctor if it becomes a problem." Kodi nodded her understanding as they left the room.

"They wore us out before the waxing so we won't have the energy to curse so much." Tally's words brought a smile to the lips of their escort, and Reagan suspected the smart-mouthed doctor was right.

"Stop bitching. At least you get to drink the good stuff. I'm stuck with regular juice. Taz has found all my stash of ginger ale and locked it up. Thank God Koi taught me how to pick locks or I'd be homicidal by now." Since they were all three in one large room separated only by curtains, they continued their conversation intermittently.

Reagan listened as the technician explained the products she'd be using and what Rafe had ordered. She felt her cheeks heat when she realized the young woman was going to be seeing pink bits only her doctor had seen in the daylight. Remembering Rafe's instruction to enjoy the refreshments, she didn't hesitate to down a margarita in record time.

"Hey, Reagan, what did you get to drink?" Tally's question sounded from the cubicle to her right just before she let out a whoop followed by a string of curses that would make any sailor proud. "Son of a fucking bitch. That's my ass you know...yanking hair out by the roots shouldn't begin there."

"A very small margarita and I want another before YEOW. Ric-Rack. Mother of God, skip the margaritas and just bring me the tequila." Reagan's crotch was on fire, and the demon masquerading as her esthetician smiled like the damned Cheshire cat. Reagan blinked her eyes to clear the watery tears, certain the woman had sprouted horns for a few seconds. "Kodi, did you see the background checks on the woman smearing wax on my pink bits? Are you sure she's a real person?"

The sweet girl with the beverage cart handed her another drink. Reagan took a huge gulp before the next strip of hide was ripped from her body. Thankfully, this drink was much stronger than the last. She might not be able to walk out of the spa, but at least the alcohol was starting to numb the pain.

"Jesus, Joseph, and Mary, have a heart, will ya? I swear I'm starting laser treatments as soon as the baby is born. This is for the birds." Reagan didn't have the heart to tell Kodi that hair grew faster during pregnancy, so she'd be back here sooner than normal for the next several months.

By the time she was bald from the waist down, Reagan had ingested more alcohol than she'd had in the previous five years combined. "I haven't drinked this much since college days my. Wait. That didn't sound right. Drank. That's is. I drank a lot. There. Better, yes?"

"Yes, indeed. That sounded better to me. I'm a bitter drinker...no, better...yes, that. I'm better at drinking than me." Reagan heard a loud clatter from Tally's side of the curtain followed by a string of curses that made her giggle. "Fuck a waddler, the floor was a lot farther down than it looked. Must have been an obstacle illusion."

"Oh boy, I'm starting to see why my Masters won't leave me unattended after I leave here." Kodi's giggle was contagious, and Reagan found herself laughing even though she didn't really understand what was so funny. "I think you mean an optical illusion, Tally."

"Yeah, that, too. What's next on our agenda? And it better not be yoga, or I'm going to fall asleep on the mat."

"I'm not doing any more yoga today. Let them give me a demerit. Fuck it. I didn't get to drink any of the good stuff, and I need a nap."

When they all banded together, refusing to return to

the yoga studio, they were led to the massage tables. "Now this is what I'm talking about. I'm looking forward to being pampered after two rounds with demons." The small sandwiches they'd eaten after their waxing had absorbed enough of the alcohol that the room finally stopped spinning and Tally was making more sense. *Shit, I bet I wasn't any better.*

"Well, you better enjoy it while you can. I saw Tabby typing on her phone like a wild woman when we didn't go back to yoga again. I'm sure she ratted us out, but honest to God, I just can't work up the energy to care." Kodi's words faded until the last few were barely a whisper.

"Bet she's out like a light. Pregnant women need more rest during the first and third trimester. She better be writing like crazy woman during those middle months because I'm dying to find out what becomes of Trish in her last book." Reagan had enjoyed the books Kodi sent her, but couldn't say she was a fan of cliffhangers.

"I keep threatening to break into her laptop to get a sneak peek, but she said she'd kill me off in her next series, and I'm just superstitious enough to worry."

Reagan giggled. "I don't care if a book has a cliffhanger, but I like to know in advance so I'm not blindsided. I've read a lot of erotic fiction, but this is the first time I've known the author, and it was easy to see Nate and Taz inspired her first book."

The conversation faded under the competent hands of their masseurs. Reagan was able to stay awake, but it was a continual struggle. By the time she was finished, her arms and legs felt like wet noodles. "Hell's bells, I'm not sure I'm going to be able to walk."

"At least we have a legitimate excuse for skipping the next round with Tabby the Torturer."

"Point taken. Off we go to hair and nails. I'm starting to feel like we're those three guys on the Wizard of Oz that go through the Wizard's stuffing and buffing line." Kodi's observation wasn't that far off track, and Reagan gained a new level of respect for the woman's imagination.

By the time she'd had her hair highlighted and trimmed and her fingernails and toenails painted, Reagan had consumed enough margaritas to make walking a straight line virtually impossible. She and Tally were like a couple of steel balls in a pinball machine as they made their way down the hallway toward the entrance. Stepping into the reception area, they were greeted by a wall of Doms.

"How many do you see?" Tally's question made Reagan giggle as she tried to focus and count the number of men standing shoulder to shoulder with their arms crossed over their chests.

"Four? No, three. Yes, definitely three, with one fading in and out." She stared for a moment before adding, "You know, that's a pretty neat trick. I wonder how he does that? I'll bet he'd do good on one of those talent shows."

"Only three, huh? Damn, I got more than that. I might need help getting home."

"Yes, *ma poupée*, I believe you will." Koi's voice didn't sound menacing, but Reagan saw Tally shudder.

"Hey, big brother. Be nice to Tally. She probably doesn't know which one of the blurry figures blocking the door is you."

"Ayasha, do not taunt your brother." Reagan tried to hone in on which figure was speaking since she'd recognized Nate's voice. At least she could identify one of the men.

"I'm the little sister. That position comes with certain rights, rights I have enjoyed my entire life, and I don't plan on relinquishing them anytime in the future." Kodi's indignant response brought identical growls from both ends of the man wall.

"Baby, we're keeping track of all the punishments you've got coming." Taz's voice was warm, but filled with warning Reagan thought was wasted effort, even if he was the figure fading in and out.

"She didn't get any of the good stuff, Master Taz, so you should give her a break." Tally leaned forward and whispered to the man Reagan was certain was Koi. "Being preggers sounds like fun until it's spa day. Then it sucks big green donkey kicks...picks...damn, penises."

Reagan couldn't hold in the laughter that bubbled to the surface. "Big green donkey dicks. Holy crap on a cactus, I haven't heard that expression since college. This was the best afternoon ever. Thanks so much for entertaining me." Looking up at Nate, she smiled, "The ladies here were nice and didn't say anything about my scars. But that Tabby person is evil." She was sure he smiled, but it was hard to tell with his face fading in and out of focus. Whispering behind her hand, she snickered, "I just thought you should know."

Someone's hand wrapped around her upper arm as they moved out of the spa, but Reagan was so focused on putting one foot in front of the other she didn't dare look to the side to see who it was. "It's Master Taz, Reagan. I'll be the one taking you home. Nate drew the short straw and is our grumpy wife's escort upstairs."

I'm not gonna say a thing. Nope, that's a trap. Just keep walking. One foot in front of the other. Don't fall down. Falling would be bad. See, there's the car, not very much farther. Shhh...be quiet, remember, Taz can hear people.

She heard Taz snort as he seated her in the car. After

she made several attempts to secure her seatbelt, he brushed her hands aside and fastened it for her, his lips pressed tightly together the entire time. She watched him in the rearview mirror as he rounded the back of the car and burst out laughing. Embarrassment assailed her, and she dropped her head into her hands. *Close your eyes…maybe he'll think you're asleep.*

Chapter Nineteen

Tally could practically feel the sexual tension pulsing in the air around Koi. He'd ushered her into the club and straight up the stairs. She wasn't sure what he had planned, but personally, she'd been hoping for something a little more social than a *wham, bam, thank you, ma'am* play session. Before Koi opened the door to one of the private rooms, he turned to her. *"Ma poupée,* I know you understand the club's rules pertaining to private rooms."

It hadn't been a question, but his pause had her answering anyway. "Yes, Sir. I do." He gave her a quick nod, and she was sure his lips had quirked in a smile, but it was gone before she'd been sure.

"Tonight, I'm suspending the rules for an hour." Her confusion must have reflected in her expression, because he grinned before pressing a kiss against her forehead. She was grateful the alcohol she'd consumed at the spa was quickly working its way out of her system. "We're going to spend the next hour talking."

Worry spiked in her as her imagination ran wild. Was he that annoyed that she'd been drinking with Reagan? Had he decided to go back to Texas? Maybe he wasn't enjoying being a third as much as she'd thought he was. *Holy hell, what if he thinks the sex sucks and he's going to tell me*

I'm too mouthy? God knows I'm not the best submissive around.

"*Ma poupée*, stop. You're overthinking this. I just want to spend time talking to you and give the alcohol time to abate before we play." She let out the breath she hadn't realized she was holding before nodding. Taking her hand in his, he tugged her close and opened the door. "Come."

Tally stepped inside and gasped. She'd been in this room numerous times, but she'd never seen it like this. The canopy bed was draped in tiny, white fairy lights that glowed softly. The spanking bench that usually took up one corner of the room had been replaced by a round table covered with a white tablecloth with three crystal candlesticks holding white tapers. Their fire reflected in the glass of a large bay window she hadn't even known was there.

Koi held out her chair, and Tally was shocked to find herself seated when she didn't remember crossing the room. Looking down, she trailed her finger along the edge of the rose pattern china and felt tears fill her eyes when she realized the antique dishes were her grandmother's. "How did you get these?"

"Karl wrapped them up and brought them to the club before he left. He knew I was planning this, and he wanted to help make the memory as sweet as possible." Koi watched her from his seat across from her. The candlelight flickered in his dark eyes, and she wondered how she'd been so lucky to find two men as thoughtful as the one she'd married and the one they'd invited into their lives.

Before she could speak, there was a soft knock at the door. Koi made his way across the room, and she admired the economy of his movements as he opened the door, smiling when she remembered Kodi telling her his name meant panther. It seemed fitting since he moved with a cat-like grace she'd noted all Special Forces soldiers seemed to possess. Randy, one of the club's bartenders, wheeled a cart into the room. The male sub didn't seem surprised by the changes that surrounded her, making her suspect he and his Mistress had helped with the redecorating.

Whatever was hidden under the silver domes on the cart smelled heavenly. Her stomach growled so loud Randy grinned, giving her a quick wink as he slipped silently from the room. Turning her attention to Koi, she was surprised to see him leaning against the large oak armoire watching her. He didn't say anything for several minutes, and she finally realized what he was waiting for.

"It smells wonderful. I hadn't realized how hungry I was until the food arrived." She'd forgotten the regular rules for the private rooms had been suspended while they enjoyed her dinner. Guessing he'd been waiting for her to remember what he'd said just before they'd entered, she tried to relax.

"Very good, sweetheart. As much as I appreciate a submissive who understands the rules, I want to enjoy another side of you for a bit. If you and I don't build a relationship outside of the one defined by D/s, there will be very little to sustain us through any separation that might occur due to my work."

"Have you accepted the Wests' offer? Will you be working with the Prairie Winds Team?" She'd heard he'd been approached, but hadn't heard that he'd made a decision. He didn't immediately return to his seat. Instead, he stood behind her for several long seconds, rubbing her shoulders. "Holy Mother of God, that feels so good. I think perhaps you missed your calling."

Koi pressed a kiss against the top of her head and moved around the table. Seating himself, he took a long drink of water from the stem glass. "My options are fairly limited right now. I can go back to work for Uncle Sam knowing I'll spend the rest of my career stuck behind a desk, or I can accept the training position Kent and Kyle have offered me."

She already suspected why he would only be working as a trainer, but she waited quietly for him to continue. "I haven't regained a full range of motion or all of the strength in my leg since the accident. The doctors aren't convinced I ever will."

Lifting her glass to meet his, she grinned. "Let me assure you, physicians are only human and, therefore, fallible. And most don't have a lot of experience with members of the Special Forces." During the earliest part of her career, she'd operated on several Army Rangers and Navy SEALs. The common denominator was their commitment to rejoining their teams, so she'd learned to never underestimate them.

His smile was equal parts friendly and hot as hell. It stole her breathe, and she hoped he hadn't seen the fine tremor in her fingers before she could return them to her lap. Lifting the domed silver lids from the food, he served her generous helpings Italian fare. He chuckled when he looked up at her. *"Ma poupée*, you are practically bouncing in your seat. You can thank my brother-in-law for sending me to your favorite eatery."

"Aha, you must be talking about Nate, since he and I enjoy teasing one another when we've been lucky enough to eat at Tony's." They spent the rest of the meal discussing exactly what his new job would look like, and she was pleased to hear he still planned to work toward returning to field work. She didn't relish the idea of him being in danger, but she understood all too well how hard it was to set aside one's passion.

Everyone had been tip-toeing around her for several weeks, and it was annoying as hell to think they didn't give her enough credit for knowing what was coming. She'd known for a year that her husband was going to ask her to move back to Washington. What she didn't know was how she was going to tell him no.

TAZ FELT EYES on him the moment they stepped from the club. Thankfully, Reagan kept him entertained enough he had no trouble pretending to be distracted. Once they were both safely ensconced inside his car, Taz cautioned his inebriated passenger to continue feigning sleep while he dialed Phoenix.

"I just left the back of the club with Reagan, and we're being watched. Where is our target?" He saw her stiffen, but to her credit, Reagan didn't move an inch. Switching his attention to her, his tone reflected his concern as he encouraged, "You're doing great, sweetie. Hold absolutely still while I move you away from the window." He moved her toward himself, settling her on the console between them. He didn't brush the hair away from her face, hoping it would allow her to hide any reaction she couldn't hold back.

"The rental car is still sitting on the street in front of his cousin's house. But thanks to your applicant, I was able to tag Merrett's phone. It's about a quarter mile behind the club and moving to the road. I assume he plans to follow you. Take the scenic route." *The scenic route? What the hell?* "I'm going to call Calamity. She's close to Rafe's house working. If I can get her in position, we'd have a hell of an advantage. That girl missed her calling. She should have been a sniper."

Taz started the car and grinned. Calamity was the nickname the Morgan boys had given Caila when they were all kids, because trouble seemed to find her no matter what she was up to. The petite vet was also a hunter and fearless when it came to anything requiring ammo. Taz remembered she'd saved Phoenix and Mitch's wife's life with a single rifle shot under almost impossible conditions, so he understood his friend's faith in her.

"Will she have a weapon with her?" As soon as he asked the question, he heard Phoenix's chuckle, and a sense of amusement washed over him as he picked up the other man's emotion.

"She'll have it. Cal doesn't go anywhere without that rifle. Well, except shopping with Mom. Mom, who put her foot down when Calamity was still in junior high." Taz could hear a flurry of activity on the other end of the line but had to block a lot of his connection with Phoenix because the man's mind moved at a dizzying rate. He'd learned a long time ago that driving while tapped into Phoenix Morgan's mind was too damned distracting to be safe.

"Just FYI, the cousin is clean—fucking squeaky clean. He'll be a good Dom. As soon as this is over, I suggest you approve his application." Taz and Nate had already decided to approve Matt's application. His interview had been one of the easiest Taz had ever done, but he wasn't entirely convinced the man was a Dom. Time would tell.

Once they were well away from the club, Taz let Reagan sit up, but cautioned her to stay low in her seat. Her eyes were clearer now than they had been a few minutes earlier. It always amazed him how fast adrenaline could counteract alcohol. She was far from sober, but she would certainly be able to run if she had to.

Phoenix interrupted his thoughts to let him know Nate had been apprised of the situation and was making calls. Taz snorted. "Goddess, he'll have a fucking army put together in ten minutes."

"Yeah, I've got a brother like that. Sage can pull people together more efficiently than Uncle Sam." Taz agreed. He'd seen the eldest Morgan brother in action, and no one could get results like Sage Morgan. Nate was efficient, but his manner was much more military. Sage, on the other hand, pulled business and personal associates together with an air of confidence seen in men born into power. From what Taz could tell, Sage had simply upped their father's game.

"I've seen Sage in action and agree. Hell, he and Nate together would be unstoppable."

"I don't even want to fucking think about it." Phoenix sounded distracted, and Taz shook his head at the man's ability to multi-task. Dusk was quickly being replaced by complete darkness. Taz usually loved how quickly night fell in the mountains, but it wasn't playing in their favor tonight. "Kip is crapping cats because I've got Caila looking for a position in the trees behind Rafe's. She'll find the best line of sight into the main part of the house. If Reagan leaves the back drapes open, it'll be an easy take-down." After a few seconds of silence, Phoenix's voice came over the speakers again. "Looks like Merrett is headed to the airport."

Reagan's head swiveled in his directions so quickly he wondered if she'd get whiplash. "Why would he go to the airport?" Her emotions were battling the alcohol still coursing through her system, and Taz reached over and grasped her hand. He didn't usually touch people who were upset because their feelings—good or bad—often swamped him. He'd known Reagan for several months, had often been able to connect with her, and was aware of how traumatized she'd been by the attack. He'd been damned impressed with her work ethic. Even Mistress Anne had mentioned what a hard worker Reagan was. And despite the fact she'd already been working full-time elsewhere, she'd never missed work.

"I'm not going to speculate on what that prick might be thinking, sweetie. What I am going to do is get you back to Rafe's and ask you to pack an overnight bag." Rafe had said he wanted to be here when Reagan found out how the woman she'd considered a friend had betrayed her, so Taz wasn't going to tell her unless it became absolutely necessary.

"Is something amiss with the security system?" Taz appreciated the fact she'd phrased her objection so tactfully, though he hadn't missed the steel in her tone. Damn, little minx had just sliced the air with a double-edged sword. If he made her leave, he'd give her the impression the security wasn't up to par. And if he let her stay, Rafe would probably have a stroke. *God dammit to hell, Rafe needs to get his ass back here.*

Taz had forgotten Phoenix was still on the line until he heard the other man chuckle. "Well done, Reagan. I'm not sure I've ever known Taz to be stunned into silence. And damn if that didn't sound exactly like something my wife would say."

"Thank you...I think." Reagan's grin belied the quiver of uncertainty he'd heard in her voice.

"Aspen is a hell of a strategist, so take it as a compliment." Taz gave her hand a squeeze and let it go when he saw some of the starch leave her spine.

"I'd prefer to stay at Master Rafe's. I promise to keep my phone close. I've imposed so much on everyone. I really want to spend what's left of the evening vegging out in front of his massive television watching something that doesn't require any thinking on my part and eating popcorn. I have every confidence in the security system, and you all will probably know before I do if there's a problem."

Twenty minutes later, Taz was back on the road, scrambling to defend his decision to Rafe, Nate, and everyone else with a fucking cell phone. "Listen, Nate, the bottom line is I can't force Reagan to come home with me. She is old enough to make her own decisions, and my role as her employer doesn't cover living arrangements. Did I want to leave her alone? Hell, no. The only other option was to stay with her. She vetoed that idea before I'd even finished offering—something about impropriety."

Taz hadn't agreed with her assessment, but he'd respected the reasoning. She didn't want to do anything that might jeopardize her budding friendship with Kodi or what she hoped might develop with Rafe. Her concern about how Rafe would feel had been the only reason his friend had stopped complaining about the fact she was now alone in his home. "Rafe, your house has better security than most military installations—she'll be fine until you get here tomorrow evening. I talked to Phoenix a few minutes ago, and she is doing exactly what she said she wanted to do—watching mindless television and eating popcorn. She has her laptop sitting beside her waiting for you to call."

"Where is the fucker now?"

"I don't know, and Phoenix was too busy tracking him to talk more than a few seconds when I called to check on

Reagan." Rafe was off the phone by the time Taz parked behind the club. He was anxious to get upstairs to Kodi, but he was going to make sure everything was running smoothly before heading up to check on her. It was still early. Most of the action at the club took place after ten o'clock. Since it was Friday night, Taz wanted to make sure the staff was ready for the influx of members anxious to shake off the tension of a long work week. With a little bit of luck, he'd be upstairs in an hour.

Chapter Twenty

RAFE WAS PLEASED when Reagan answered his computer call on the second ring. He'd seen the iPad lying on the table in front of her on the security feed, but he hadn't expected her to practically fall off the sofa trying to pull it on to her lap before it could ring a second time. "Hello, beautiful. How was your spa day?" He'd heard the thread of anxiety when she'd answered, and he hated that she was dealing with everything alone.

"Oh, it was amazing…well, most of it was." Rafe laughed out loud at her unintentional confession. Since he already spoken to Taz, he'd been updated on the ladies' day and Reagan's reaction to the full Brazilian wax he'd scheduled for her. Damn, he could hardly wait to feel her smooth pussy lips. He planned to bury his face between her legs and not surface for hours.

"What part was the most challenging, Peach?" She squirmed in her seat, and he saw the pink blush bloom over her chest and spread upward. "Reagan, I asked you a question, and I expect an answer. When a Dom asks a question, he doesn't want you to edit your response. I don't want you to give me the answer you think I want, nor do I want you to give me an answer you believe makes you look better." She blinked her eyes several times, and he assumed the alcohol was still creating enough brain fog she wasn't processing his words as quickly as usual.

"It has always amazed me how this very simple rule creates such a challenge for submissives—particularly the really bright ones. Their minds are always working, so information rarely slides free without moving through a plethora of filters." Her eyes were glazed over, but he could have sworn the corners of her lips turned up ever so slightly. Damn, he hated doing this remotely. It would be so much easier to read her if they were sitting side by side or, better yet, she was sitting naked on his lap with his dick shoved balls deep in her heat. It was damned hard for a sub to hide anything in that position.

"What was the most challenging part, Reagan?" This time his words were tight, and he'd almost ground them out from behind his clenched jaw.

The change of tone seemed to jar her from whatever mental road trip her brain had taken, and she answered immediately. "The waxing, Sir."

"Much better. Was the pain too much for you to endure?" He was certain that wasn't the case—God knew she'd endured far worse in the past.

She shook her head vehemently as she spoke. "No. The pain was manageable; the margaritas helped a lot."

"Then what made the experience so difficult?"

The pink staining her cheeks turned scarlet, but this time she didn't hesitate. "It was weird and embarrassing having a stranger touch me…there."

"There? Come on, Reagan. You're a medical professional. You can do better than that." Yes, he understood exactly what she was saying, but damned if he wasn't enjoying watching her squirm. Too bad she wasn't impaled on his cock. He'd be enjoying that squirm infinitely more.

She raised her eyes to meet his, and he saw a flash of

fire in them that made his cock instantly ramrod stiff. At times over the past couple of weeks, Rafe had wondered if there was any fire left in Reagan—she'd seemed completely defeated these past few days. But his hope soared when he saw there was indeed an iron will deep inside her.

"A woman I didn't know smeared hot wax all over my pubis, the outer regions of my nether lips, and around my anus. Then this virtual stranger applied cloth strips, patting them down with a touch far too personal for someone I'd only been introduced to minutes earlier. After a few minutes spent rubbing the strips ensuring *good adhesion*, she ripped the strips off, yanking all the hair out by the roots. Keep in mind this woman wasn't a *medical professional,* and hell, that would have been humiliating enough. No, this was a woman you'd paid to touch me intimately, and I'm still trying to sort through how I feel about the money element."

Her words had spilled out so quickly Rafe doubted she'd have been able to hold back the torrent even if she'd wanted to. But now, he could see the uncertainty in her eyes. She always expected rejection—and damned if that didn't royally piss him off. Oddly, he wasn't angry that she'd turned his own words around on him mockingly. No, it was her expectation of being set out on the curb like yesterday's garbage that annoyed him.

"Wipe that worried look off your face, Peach. I asked you for an honest answer, and that is exactly what you gave me. The humor I found in it was a bonus." Her shoulders relaxed, but he intended to enjoy the remnants of her unease before it all faded away. "Now that I know the experience made you uncomfortable, I'd like to see if it was worth it. Strip and show me every inch of your bare sex."

She looked around, and he growled. "There is no one there but you, baby, and you just earned ten. You're going to rack up an impressive number of stokes if you're not careful, baby. I'm not sure your ass is going to be able to endure them all in one session." She didn't know he'd asked Phoenix to cut the feed from the living room for the next hour. He intended to use this as a lesson in trust—the first in what he suspected would be many more to come.

"Do you trust me, Reagan?" It was a simple question, but he could see the meaning wasn't lost on her.

"Yes, Sir. I don't really know why or how exactly when that happened...but I do trust you."

He didn't respond, just nodded his acceptance of her answer and watched as she propped the iPad against the back of the sofa and stepped in front of the screen. Pulling her faded Scooby Doo® t-shirt over her head, she tossed it aside, and he groaned aloud. "You are so beautiful, and I can hardly wait to get my mouth on those lovely nipples. Before you lose the pants, turn for me...very slowly." From what he could see during her slow-motion pirouette, she'd healed even faster than he'd hoped. The instructions he'd give her masseuse had detailed exactly how much pressure could be used on her healing scars, and he was pleased to see none of them appeared to be enflamed or swollen.

"Now the pants, baby. I'm hard as a rock thinking about how sweet you're going to taste. You'll be so much more sensitive. Every slide of my tongue against the petals of your sex will light you up like the Fourth of July." Her fingers were trembling as she reached for the waistband of her sweats. Almost every piece of clothing he'd seen her wear was in tatters, but he bit back the observation. He wanted nothing more than to lavish her with gifts, but they weren't *there* yet. She'd interpret any negative comment about her wardrobe as a potential excuse to send her on her way, and he wasn't giving her anything to stew about.

He smiled when he realized she wasn't wearing any panties. "I'm happy to see you followed the esthetician's advice and skipped panties this evening, baby. You might as well get used to the breeze wafting over you. I will keep you naked at every opportunity. And even when you are dressed, you'll have little need for undergarments when we're together." She paused as a shiver seemed to race up her spine.

When the fabric disappeared from his sight, he let her settle before pushing her. "Sit on the coffee table and spread your legs. I want to be able to see everything." While she moved into position, he added, "I'll call you from the airport tomorrow. That will give you time to light the fireplace behind you. I want you naked and kneeling with your hands resting on your wide-spread thighs so that your bare sex is directly in my line of sight when I step through the door."

He didn't want to overwhelm her with information, but Rafe bit back a grin thinking about how familiar she was going to become with the position. There would be evenings when he posed her on a table and did nothing but look at her. Nate and Taz had used Kodi as a table decoration during a play party a few months ago. It had been a punishment for some minor infraction, but he wasn't sure who'd suffered the most. The little sub who'd been fondled by every one of the party's guests or her Masters who hadn't considered how difficult it would be to see their naked woman being aroused by their friends.

Reagan wasn't tall, and at six foot three, Rafe dwarfed her. But he loved her lean, athletic build. Her legs were long and nicely toned, and he was anxious to see them spread wide on a St. Andrew's cross. The one he'd installed in his personal play room used hydraulics to tilt a bound submissive in a variety of positions. He looked forward to having her spread wide for his pleasure as he introduced a whole new level of discipline into her life. Reagan wouldn't believe him now, but she'd find a level of confidence she'd never known before when she learned to truly surrender.

"Thank you for sharing your beautiful body with me tonight, even if it has left me with a raging hard on." He loved hearing her sweet giggle. He wanted to end their conversation on a more casual note. "You can put your clothes on as soon as we end this call. The living room cameras will be turning back on in five minutes. Get some sleep, Peach. You're going to need it tomorrow." The last thing he saw before he closed the window was her blowing him a kiss. He doubted she'd intended for him to see her, but he was glad he'd looked up in time to catch a fleeting glimpse of her spontaneous, sweet gesture.

Making his way to the shower, Rafe wondered if taking himself in hand would provide any relief. He suspected the image of Reagan's bare sex playing on continuous loop in his head was going to fuel his libido longer than the hot water would last.

REAGAN'S ENTIRE BODY felt like it was tremoring at the very center of her being. The pulses deep in her core vibrated their way to the surface. Rafe hadn't even been able to touch her, and she was more aroused than she'd ever been…it didn't make any sense. She'd dressed and was already moving down the hall when the living room lights flashed behind her. Chuckling to herself, she didn't bother looking for one of the well-concealed cameras. She just grinned and thanked Master Phoenix for the heads-up. Over the past couple of days, she'd accepted the fact she was being watched. But it was Kodi's comment earlier today that sealed the deal.

"Sister, you need to look at this differently. Think of it as having a roomie. You share all the common areas of the house, but still have your private space. It should be comforting to know that while Master Rafe is in San Francisco you aren't alone up here in the foothills." Kodi's simple observation changed everything. Viewing their observation as friendly rather than intrusive, would make her life much easier. They'd even worked out a communication system of sorts. Rather than having them speak to her directly, she'd respectfully asked them to simply make the lights flicker off and back on once for yes or twice for no. Just before Rafe called, she'd waved and the lights had flickered several times, letting her know whoever was watching was acknowledging her gesture.

As strange as it seemed, it was comforting knowing she had a guardian angel. Someday, she'd asked to meet the people who were watching over her. By the time she slipped between the sheets, her eyelids were already sliding closed. The alcohol had faded, but the fatigue of the adrenaline crash still lingered. She'd forced herself to stay awake until after Rafe's call, and now that it was over, she was sliding rapidly toward the bliss of sleep when she heard her phone vibrate on the side table.

The message from Rafe was short and to the point…it also launched her from sleepy to hot in the time it took her to read it.

Remove your pajamas, Peach. You will always be bare when sleeping in my bed, whether I'm with you or not. Let every brush of the sheets against your sweet pink nipples be a prelude. And remember how cool the cotton is against your luscious ass, because tomorrow night, those lovely round globes will wear my marks.

Her body lit up from the inside, and after slipping the shirt over her head, Reagan's mind registered each brush of the Egyptian cotton against her bare skin. The nerve endings awakened, making her crave the touch she wouldn't have until he returned tomorrow. Maybe she'd use her fingers to find a bit of relief. No one would know. The room was shrouded in darkness, and she was under the covers. No one would be the wiser.

The temptation had barely finished floating through mind when her phone rattled on the table again.

Remember, your pussy belongs to me. It's mine to pleasure, mine to touch. You do not have permission to play with what belongs to me. You'll be punished for stealing pleasure. And trust me, baby, I will know.

Chapter Twenty-One

KELSEY KICKED THE rolling stool across the open area in the freight company's back room, cursing a blue streak when her toe connected with the metal. She was frustrated, tired, and pissed. And fuck it all if she didn't have to add careless to the list now. Her boss had almost fired her for leaving early last night, but she'd gotten spooked when the security system started acting up and bailed. And since she'd been in his office getting the mother of all ass-chewings, she hadn't been able to get her package on the last flight out today and had been forced to volunteer to work late so she could slip it on to the first flight out tomorrow morning. The drugs would be hours late arriving, but at least they would be delivered. Her contact loved reminding her that failure was not an option.

"That's the reason I don't let my staff wear open-toed shoes." The words came from behind her, and Kelsey turned so quickly she almost fell into a heap of tangled arms and legs. Holy shit, how had he gotten in without setting off the alarms? Dammit, was the fucking system messing up again tonight? She recognized him immediately, and a white-hot bolt of fear raced up her spine. "I don't know why you look so surprised, Kelsey. You had to know I'd find you."

"I didn't tell you where I was." She hated the catch she

heard in her voice. The man standing in front of her didn't look like anyone she'd want to tangle with. As she edged closer to the door, her eyes moved to the camera and for the first time since she'd worked there, Kelsey hoped the security company was paying attention. His laughter boomed around her, and she felt her blood run cold. "You don't think I left the security feeds operational, do you? Kelsey, dear, you are not dealing with the local mountain bumpkin sheriff."

"You know Brandt Morgan?" Dammit, she probably shouldn't have given the man that information.

"Yes and no. I know he started poking his nose into my business within hours of our conversation. I didn't know who he was at first, but once I'd tracked you down, it didn't take long to figure out who was asking questions." The smile he gave her was more of a sneer, and it sent chills racing up her arms.

"What kind of questions? I don't know why he'd be asking about you."

"You're a lousy liar, Ms. Jones. I think you know exactly why he started asking questions. Or should I say, he had his friends grilling anyone who'd take their calls." It wasn't until her back connected with the cold steel door that Kelsey realized he'd been matching her step for step. For each step she'd taken back, he'd taken one forward, always keeping the distance between them the same…until now. He continued forward until he was close enough for her to see the fury simmering in his eyes.

Her first instinct was to run, but before she'd taken the second step, Merrett's hands were wrapped around her neck. She fought to pull in oxygen, terrified each breath she took would be her last as she felt her feet leave the ground. "Where is Reagan? I saw her leaving the local kink club with her Native American boyfriend, but I couldn't get to the car fast enough to follow them." *Native American boyfriend?* "I'm tired of seeing that phony confused look, bitch. Tell me where she is—right fucking now." Darkness began creeping in from the periphery of her vision, and its progression accelerated as his grip tightened.

She could barely breathe, and she wasn't going to waste any air speaking. Her mind skittered to his comment about Reagan having a Native American boyfriend making her wonder what had happened with Rafe? Had he figured out how boring Reagan was? Kelsey felt like she was floating, and the last thing she heard was his vicious profanity-laced threats and the faint sound of a siren in the distance.

PHOENIX STARED AT the large screen in front of him, tracking Merrett's phone. The small green indicator showed the man approaching the back door of the freight company, but just as he turned his attention to the monitor on his right, it went black. "What the fuck?"

"What happened?" Brandt's voice came over the speakers, and Phoenix heard the frustration in his voice.

"The security feed from the freight company just went down."

"Switch to another cam."

"Yeah, well, big brother, shocking as it may seem, I'd actually thought of that. When I say it's down, I mean the whole fucking system is down. I don't have shit." The only way the man could have disabled the system that fast was by using a scrambler. Running the feed backwards ten minutes, he watched Kelsey Jones move around the room and stealthily avoid the cameras she and the other employees had been told covered the large room. What no one except the owner knew was that he'd recently added several more cameras. Brandt hadn't had any trouble obtaining a warrant, and the two of them had finished the installation late last night after the system experienced a brief malfunction.

"Did you get anything before everything went dark?"

"Yes. You'll have plenty to make an arrest." *If she's still alive when you get there.* "What's your ETA?" He needed to know Brandt's estimated time of arrival to gauge how much help to bring in to help track Merrett. No doubt the man could hear the siren. Sounds that shrill tended to echo up and down the valley in the most annoying way possible. If an emergency vehicle was far enough north, they could hear it at the ranch, and it always woke up every baby in the damned house.

"Five minutes unless I come up behind another hay trailer. Damn, I hate this time of year." Brandt was the most impatient driver in the world, which was damned amusing considering he was the lead law enforcement agent in the county. Phoenix could hear Brandt speaking to central dispatch, requesting ambulance and officer back up. Before he'd finished his instructions, he let loose a string of curses that would send their mother into a tailspin. In Phoenix's opinion, she was awfully thin-skinned for the mother of five boys.

He didn't have to wait long to find out what had set Brandt off. Phoenix heard the distinctive click of Brandt opening the link so that his officers and dispatcher could hear everything Phoenix heard. "I was almost run off the road by a car matching the one owned by the suspect's cousin." He gave a quick description of the car and directed officers to pursue and detain.

Phoenix dialed Caila on another line. "Hey, doll, are you still working down by Rafe's?" He let a sigh of relief when she said she was just leaving the area.

"I'll be in place in ten minutes tops. What's up? I can hear sirens over my radio so I know they're close." As loud as she played her music, he wouldn't have thought she'd be able to hear a nuclear explosion. "And before you ask, yes, I've got warm clothes and a night vision scope. I'm just a regular fucking boy scout."

"Har har. And you better not let Mom hear you talking like that—or Kip for that matter."

"Yeah, yeah. But you won't blab because I'm going to be sitting in a tree in the cold helping you out." *Brat.* Unfortunately, she was right. Glancing at his phone, Phoenix groaned. "What's wrong?"

"Rafe just landed. He's so anxious to get back to Reagan he's liable to jump out of the damned plane before it even comes to a stop."

"Which means he'll be coming in hot and you don't want me to screw up and shoot the wrong guy, right? Damn, that's just insulting." Phoenix could hear the amusement in her voice, but she'd been right. That was exactly what he'd been thinking. "I only shoot bad guys, Phoenix."

"I'm sorry, Cal. I just wanted to give you a heads-up because this jack ass actually bears a strong resemblance to Rafe."

"I understand that at your advanced age it's hard to distinguish differences at a distance, but I'm not pushing forty, so…"

Hell, she wasn't even thirty. "You're a menace. And

I'm only thirty-five, so I think 'pushing forty' is a bit of an exaggeration."

"You're a Mensa, so I'm sure you understand the concept of rounding numbers. Anything five or more gets rounded up. Hence, pushing forty." He heard the faint ding of her car door before she tested the earbud communication device he'd given her. The sound of her trunk closing told him she was ready to go to work. "Gotta go. Places to be. Bad guys to shoot."

"Stay safe, little sister." Opening the link between his office and Micah Drake's at the Prairie Winds Club, he updated the other man and was grateful for his offer of help. He let Micah take the helm for a few minutes while he talked to Rafe.

"Brandt found Kelsey by the back door. Looks like Merrett was choking her when he heard the sirens and fled." The son of a bitch dropped her like she was a piece of trash to be discarded. Phoenix certainly didn't respect her, but she was still a human being.

"Where are they taking her?"

"North. Tally isn't available, and Ryan has more experience with this sort of thing than the doctor on call." Rafe already knew Tally had been drinking the day before, so he'd understand why she referred the case to Ryan.

BRANDT LOOKED ON as the EMS personnel worked to save Kelsey Jones's life. If he'd been a few seconds later arriving, she'd have died. The trauma to her throat and the position in which she'd fallen would have cut off what little oxygen she'd been able to pull in. He heard the EMTs mention asphyxiation and something about hypoxia and made a mental note to look it up later.

He snapped a couple of quick pictures and sent them to Ryan along with anything else he thought might help his brother treat her. Even though he wanted nothing more than to see her held accountable for selling out her friend and behind bars for smuggling drugs, neither of those meant she deserved to die.

When his phone vibrated in his pocket, Brandt wasn't surprised to see a message from Ryan. *Was assailant trying to find out Reagan's location?* Brandt didn't know, but that was his best guess.

Probably.

Did he get it? Considering her earlier lack of loyalty, it was likely she'd told him everything he wanted to know—not that it appeared to have done any good.

??

DICK MERRETT COULDN'T get that bitch's last words out of his head. She'd been so frantic to escape from him, he doubted she realized she'd spoken anywhere but her clouded mind. He'd done his research. He knew Reagan worked part-time at the club. It still amazed him she was using her real name and social security number. When he'd seen her leaving the club with a man, he'd assumed the man was her boyfriend. But Kelsey seemed confused by him referring to her man as a Native American. Instead, she seemed to think Reagan was with someone named Rafe.

Looking around, he found what he was looking for—a

convenience store close to the exit for the airport. Over the years, he'd learned people are extremely predictable. They'd stop at either the place closest to their home or one near work for their caffeine fix, so this place would be a likely stop for the airport personnel.

Twenty minutes later, he could barely hide his smile as walked from the small store and settled back into his cousin's beat up old car. The young man working behind the counter had been very helpful, and his confession to having a secret crush on Dr. Rafe Newell was enlightening. He hadn't thought the man, whose nametag identified him as Treavor, was going to talk to him until Dick claimed to be Reagan's ex-boyfriend and that he'd come to town to beg her forgiveness.

"You know Reagan. She's got a such a good heart. I know she'll come back home with me if I can just talk to her." Treavor's eyes lit up when he realized how easily he could rid himself of one person he believed was keeping Newell from claiming Treavor as his own.

"I've been to the club a few times with friends and watched Master Rafe top male and female subs. He never fucks any of them, though. I think he's waiting for the right one to come along." *And I'm sure the good doctor has his sights set on you. Not.*

Treavor, the helpful clerk, had even provided directions to Rafe Newell's mountain home. Dick wanted to pat himself on the back; stopping at the convenience store had been a stroke of genius. Making the turn that would take him up the mountain, Dick looked in the rearview mirror in time to see an ambulance fly by, lights flashing and the siren piercing the air. He'd been sure the bitch was dead, but some well-meaning EMT probably thought they'd be a hero if they managed to revive her. Shrugging it off, he remembered the housing development he'd passed on the way into town. *One of the old farts up there probably had a heart attack trying to breathe.* This was one of the reasons he loved Texas. No fucking altitude sickness.

The mountains might be pretty to look at; the air was entirely too thin. Damn, even the smallest physical exertion was exhausting. He hoped Newell's home wasn't too far up the mountain. Dick had his heart set on fucking Reagan before he finished what the dirt bag in his facility was supposed to have completed over a year ago, and keeling over from heart failure for a piece of ass wasn't part of his plan.

Chapter Twenty-Two

REAGAN SHIVERED, BUT it didn't have anything to do with the wind howling outside the enormous windows of Rafe's home. When she'd spoken with him this morning, Rafe had directed her to the master control panel for the security system. He'd talked her through disabling the speakers and the cameras for the main living area. She'd felt the oddest sense of freedom knowing she finally had a bit of privacy. Maybe she hadn't been as sold on Kodi's roommate idea as she'd thought?

Excitement threatened to bubble over, and she fought the urge to run back to the bedroom to retrieve her ringing phone. Kneeling naked with her back to the fireplace, Reagan was wedged between the long sofa and the overstuffed chair she loved curling up in to read. Rechecking her position, she adjusted her knees so they were as far apart as she could get them. She let her gaze move quickly over her immediate surroundings. Spotting something silver under the sofa cushion, Reagan almost groaned when she realized she hadn't properly returned the small pistol to its original hiding place.

Rafe had quizzed her several times to make sure she could confidently operate the small Sig Sauer P938. He wanted to be absolutely certain she was familiar with its operation. Just as she lifted her hand to push the pistol farther under the cushion, she heard the back-door open. Shocked she hadn't heard the garage door open or close, she quickly readjusted her hands on her thighs and waited.

"Well, well, well. What do we have here? Did you know I was coming, Reagan? If I'd known I'd find you naked and spread for me like the slut you are, I'd have worked harder to find you." Her blood turned to ice in her veins when she realized Major Merrett stood directly in front of her. She struggled to get to her feet, but he tangled his fingers in her hair, stilling her movement.

"Looks like your fuck-buddy did a good job of hiding all those nasty scars, bitch. Too bad he wasted his time, because I'm going to carve you up again after I sample the cunt you seem intent on sharing with everyone but me." The sinister tone of his voice sent chills racing over her bare skin. When black dots began dancing in her vision, Reagan realized she was holding her breath and sucked in a big gulp of air. The last thing she needed was to pass out, leaving herself completely defenseless.

Think, Reagan. Rafe will be here any minute. If he walks in, he'll be a sitting duck. Her Master wouldn't be expecting anyone else to be in the house, and with the cameras disabled, he'd have no way of knowing the dangerous situation that awaited him. The realization she'd accepted Rafe as her Master struck her like a blow to the chest, and her need to protect him swamped her.

As if he'd known she was lost in thought, Merrett yanked her hair so hard she fell to the side. Catching herself against the side of the sofa, Reagan let her hand slip between the cushions and wrap around the pistol's grip. Sending up a silent prayer of thanks for Rafe's insistence she learn how to use the gun, she flicked off the safety and palmed as much of the weapon as she could before pulling her hands free. From his position in front of her, he wouldn't be able to see her hand. Thank God she'd knelt between two pieces of furniture.

"You are a ditzy bitch, aren't you? Hell, I don't think you've heard a word I said. But at least you are in the perfect position to suck me. Don't fucking move."

He released her hair, and she felt herself sway with relief. Finally finding her voice, she gasped, "Cameras. There are cameras everywhere, and the police are probably already on their way."

He laughed and laid a small black box on the table behind him. "Scramblers are the best thing the geeks have invented in a long time. Took out the system at that freight company you worked for with no problem at all."

"You went there looking for me? How did you know I used to work there?"

"Your buddy Kelsey sold you out, bitch. She called me wanting money in exchange for your location. Why would I pay her when it was easy to find out who she was and where she was calling from?"

"Kelsey told you where to find me?" She hated the quivering in her voice, but the combination of fear and betrayal was almost too much for her to wrap her head around. How did she always manage to trust the wrong people? Regretting her earlier relief at having the security system turned off, she shook her head in disgust when she realized it didn't matter anyway. If he was right about the scrambler, Phoenix would have just assumed there was glitch in the system.

"Open your mouth. I'm going to fuck your throat before I take what should have been mine a year ago." The sound of his zipper shifted her entire world on its axis. Time slowed despite the fact everything seemed to happen at once. The rasp of the zipper's metal teeth releasing and the low rumble of the garage door opening shot adrenaline through her system, and Reagan's mind cleared. The fog of fear was replaced by the knowledge she not only had to save herself; she had to save Rafe as well.

Merrett's hand once again clenched her hair, yanking her head to the side. Reagan wouldn't be able to see where she was shooting, but that didn't stop her from pulling her hand from beneath her. She aimed up and pulled the trigger. His scream caused her to flinch, pulling the trigger a second time, but this shot sounded much louder…more like an explosion than a single shot from a pistol.

Glass shattered in front of her, and she instinctively covered her face. Merrett's fingers flexed before sliding from her hair. He gasped once before falling in front of her. A knife she hadn't known he was holding slid across the wood floor as Reagan scrambled back and away from the man who seconds early had been intent on shoving his cock into mouth. Shuddering when she thought about how close she'd come to being raped, Reagan screamed when warm hands wrapped around her upper arms and lifted her from the floor.

Her wild flailing was quickly stilled when she was wrapped in a soft blanket and picked up. "Shhh. I've got you, sweetheart. Just let me hold you for a little while." Rafe's voice calmed the worst of the storm churning in her as he moved across the room and fell into a chair with her still cradled in his arms. His shuddering breath matched her own, and as strange as it was, she found comfort in the fact he'd been as worried for her as she'd been for him.

What seemed like long minutes later, he leaned back and looked down at her. "Reagan, why didn't you answer your phone?"

"My phone? Oh shit."

"Oh shit, indeed." His eyes darkened, but she could tell he wasn't really angry. If she was going to make a guess, she'd venture Masters didn't enjoy feeling that out of control. "I'm not going to assign a number of swats right now. I need to calm my racing heart before I give you some astronomical number, because I'll always keep my promises, baby. But I assure you, it's going to be a paddling you won't soon forget."

The words set her on fire. The adrenaline flooding her system turned to raging desire between one heartbeat and the next. Rafe's fingers grasped her chin. Tilting her face up, he sealed his lips over hers. The kiss morphed from an assurance she was all right into a full-blown claiming before she could wiggle her arms free from the confines of the blanket. "Stay where you are, baby. I need to know you're safe." She moaned into his second kiss before he pulled back to gaze into her eyes. "I do believe bondage is something you're going to enjoy. I'm looking forward to exploring that with you."

CAILA HADN'T HESITATED to take the shot when she saw what Merrett held in his hand. The long, slender blade reminded her of a filet knife on steroids. She'd been right about the spot she'd chosen; the elevated vantage point had given her a perfect view into the room, and her scope let her track the prick stalking Reagan from the time he'd gotten out of his car. She'd wanted to shoot him then, but Brandt was a real stickler for the rules, and he'd reminded her that shooting someone before they committed a crime was against the rules. *Damn, he used to be more fun when we were kids.*

Dropping out of the tree, she laid her rifle at her feet, propped her hands on her knees, and took a deep breath. She'd seen Reagan pull the gun from between the cushions and was damned impressed when she'd taken the first shot. Unfortunately, Merrett chosen that moment to jerk Reagan so hard by the hair she'd almost fallen over. It looked like the bullet had grazed his thigh, but from his reaction, one would have thought she'd shot his cock off at the root. *What a fucking baby.*

"That was one hell of a shot, baby." Her husband's sexy voice startled her, and she jerked upright to find him leaning casually against a tree a few feet in front of her. He had a rifle slung over his shoulder, and she didn't remember a time she'd been happier to see him. Tears spilled down her cheeks as the reality of what she'd done crashed over her. "Aww, sweetheart, come here." Where had her mind been that she hadn't even heard him move? Kip's strong arms closed around her, and she let his strength seep into her.

"How long have you been here?"

"I was right behind you coming up the mountain. I had to park farther down so you were already in place before I caught up, so I took a position by the first fork in the path. The only reason I found you—great perch by the way—was because I swiped one of these from Phoenix's office the other day." She watched him pull an earbud just like hers from his ear. Caila knew exactly why he'd waited down the path…he was protecting her, and she loved him for it.

He leaned forward, pressed a kiss against her forehead, and grinned. "I can't let the Mistress of Mayhem have all the fun, you know." Caila rolled her eyes at the mention of one of the Morgan brothers' favorite nicknames for her. "Baby, did you just roll your eyes at me?" The two of them weren't as deep into the D/s dynamic as his brothers and their wives, but they did enjoy playing every once in a while.

"Actually, I was rolling my eyes at the nickname I don't believe I deserve, but if a false confession will get me a *funishment* spanking and hot sex, then I'll be all over it."

He hugged her tight before leaning down to pick up her rifle. "Come on, baby, let's go start the mountain of paperwork my brother is going to subject us to before he lets us go home to have some wild monkey sex. Mom's got all the grandkids at their house in town, so hopefully, big brother can be persuaded to delay some of his questions until tomorrow."

Caila didn't think it was likely, but she wasn't above batting her eyes and whining a little if it meant spending time doing naked mattress gymnastics with her man. She'd loved Kip since she old enough to understand what love was. Becoming his wife had been one of the happiest day of her life, because she'd not only gotten the man of her dreams, she'd gotten his family as well.

RAFE MOVED HER off his lap and settled her on the sofa when he saw Kip lead Caila into the room. "Wait here, love. I want to thank Caila."

"Thank her?"

"For saving your life, baby. The shot that took Merrett down was hers, Peach."

Reagan was stunned. "Dr. Caila Morgan? The vet?"

When Caila giggled behind him, Rafe turned and smiled down at the petite bundle of trouble and pulled her in for a quick hug. Reagan heard him thanking Caila for saving her as Kip knelt in front of the sofa. His eyes were filled with concern as he inquired, "You okay, sweetheart?"

"Yes, and I hear I have your wife to thank for that fact." Reagan was still trying to wrap her head around it.

He nodded and gave her a grin Reagan bet had melted a lot of women right out of their panties before he'd gotten married. "She's racking up an impressive resume. I hope Uncle Sam doesn't get wind of her skills."

"Oh no! Is she going to be in trouble for shooting that prick? Because if there ever was a man who deserved to be shot, it was Major Merrett."

"Hell no, I'm worried the military will try to recruit her." His laughter was contagious, and she appreciated it more than she could tell him. The dam of emotion she'd been holding back bubbled forth as that laughter switched from amusement to something far too close to hysteria for her comfort.

Caila sat next to her and wrapped her arm around Reagan's shoulders. "It's the adrenaline crash. The more you try to hold it in, the harder the fall, so let it go." The other woman's words settled over her, and Reagan was grateful for her support. Damn, it had been a long time since she'd had friends to talk to, and in the past few days, she'd been surrounded by women who offered their friendship. Not one of them had asked her for anything in return.

"Thank you. I know it's not enough, but I don't think anything would ever be enough to show my gratitude. He was going to kill me, but not until after he made me wish a thousand times for the relief of death." She shuddered, and Caila nodded her understanding. "I tried to shoot him, but the prick tried to pull my hair out by the roots, and I fell over. I was going to shoot him right in the…well, I was going to make sure Dick didn't have a dick anymore."

Caila giggled, Kip roared with laughter, and Rafe snorted a laugh even as he shook his head, looking for all the world like he couldn't believe what he'd just heard. But it was Brandt Morgan who spoke. She hadn't seen him walk up beside Kip, his dark eyes dancing with amusement. "Blood thirsty little wench, isn't she?"

"Oh yes, she's going to fit right in." Caila turned her attention to Rafe, "You'd better keep her, Sir. She and I are going to get along great. And I can hardly wait to introduce her to my sisters-in-law." Kip and Brandt groaned in unison, making Caila clap her hands looking like a little girl who'd found her heart's desire under the Christmas tree.

Brandt held up his hand, gaining everyone's attention in a way that reminded her all three men standing in front of her were sexual Dominants. Instinctively, her eyes moved to Rafe, though he wasn't the man who'd commanded their attention. His slow nod of approval launched a flurry of butterflies in her stomach. Brandt's deep voice cut through her budding arousal, "We've boarded up the window and cleaned up what we can. I want all of you in my office tomorrow morning. The reports can wait until then." Focusing his attention on Caila, Brandt's expression softened. "That was one hell of a shot, Cal. I'm damned proud of you. Hell, there were only a few guys in the SEALs who could have drilled that shot."

Reagan watched Kip when Caila whispered, "I had good teachers." His eyes were filled with a mixture of pride, love, and molten lust that made Reagan wonder if the couple would make it home before the passion steamrolled them.

Twenty minutes later, she and Rafe were the only ones left in the house. He'd led her to the bedroom before pulling the blanket from her shoulders. "Don't move." Leaving her standing beside the bed, he strode purposely across the large master bedroom to turn on the gas fireplace. She'd noticed the dark marble feature, but hadn't seen it aflame until now. When he heard her gasp, he turned and smiled. "It's beautiful, isn't it? It was my one completely extravagant addition after I bought the house."

Beautiful didn't do it justice. The flames appeared to dance atop a bed of mirrored glass. The configuration was constantly changing. One minute, it was a straight line; the next, it looked like a crowd performing the wave in the stands during a college football game. "It's amazing. I've never seen anything like it."

"I'll tell you more about it—later. Right now, I want you to turn around and lie over the edge of the bed with your legs spread more than shoulder width apart and your toes turned in." She blinked her eyes in surprise, and he cocked a brow, waiting for her to comply. "You have a safe word, Reagan. Do you want to use it?"

The question pushed her to move quickly into position. She'd been waiting too long to let uncertainty steal this moment from her. He stepped behind her, his gaze a warm caress on her chilled skin. The shattered floor to ceiling window downstairs along with the steady stream of people in and out of the house meant the temperature had dropped to nearly freezing inside. Reagan was glad she'd closed the master bedroom door earlier in the evening, retaining at least some of the heat.

"Stay with me, Peach. I don't want your mind wandering. I can be very creative when it comes to keeping subs focused." Oh, she could only imagine all the tricks he had up his sleeve. She'd kept herself busy the past couple of days reading everything she could find online about Dominance and submission. What impressed her the most was the emphasis on communication and the absolute commitment of reputable clubs to safe, sane, and consensual as the guiding tenet of the lifestyle.

A sharp slap landed on her left ass cheek, making her shriek as heat exploded over her bare skin. She instinctively started to stand and discovered his hand wrapped possessively around the back of her neck. *When did he do that?* Her reflex was no match for his strength, and a second wave of heat moved through her at the feeling of being bound by him, even if it was just his hand holding her in place.

"How interesting."

"Sir?"

"Peach, your respiration rate increased with the swat, but it was the feeling of being restrained that sent your heart rate through the roof."

"I think having a Dom who's a doctor might have some disadvantages I hadn't previously considered." She heard the quiver in her voice and there wasn't a snowball's chance in hell he'd missed it. *Damn, nothing like turning into a puddle of goo after only one swat. Nothing needy about that, no siree.*

Chapter Twenty-Three

RAFE LEANED HIS head back and laughed. Reagan's comment delighted him and he couldn't remember the last time he'd laughed during a D/s scene. How she'd managed to retain her sense of humor after everything she'd been through this evening was a mystery to him. He'd planned to paddle her ass to pull her out of the stupor he thought she'd fallen into, but damned if she hadn't just proven him wrong. Now he'd give her the five swats she'd earned a few days ago and defer the rest until tomorrow night.

The scene he was planning at the club could easily be adapted to add the additional punishment she'd earned this evening. Rafe had never hidden the fact he enjoyed meting out discipline when a submissive blatantly ignored a command, especially one given to keep the sub safe. By the time he administered the five swats he'd promised her a few moments earlier, he was confident she would still feel the remnants tomorrow morning.

Smoothing his hand over her ass cheeks, he admired their flawless round shape. "You have a beautiful ass, baby. And I love the way my handprint bloomed the perfect shade of pink. My goal is to turn your entire backside the same color as your pussy." Sliding his fingers down the crack between her cheeks, he smiled when he found her wet folds. "You're very wet, baby. I think we're going to get along splendidly. I'm going to show you just how easy it is to blur the line between pleasure and pain."

Her pussy was slick and he could smell her arousal. The folds were swelling under his touch, and he loved watching them unfold as blood flowed into the tender tissues. The mirror behind her gave him a lovely view, something he was certain would make her blush when she realized the peep show he was enjoying. Continuing to slide his fingers close, but not close enough, to her clit, he almost laughed when she subtly tried to shift from one foot to the other in an effort to get him closer to the target.

He pulled his fingers from her sex before he gave in to the temptation to finger fuck her to orgasm. She hadn't earned it, and he was determined to begin as he intended to go. "Tell me why you're being punished, Reagan." It had been so long and so much had transpired, he wondered if she'd remember. Once again, she surprised him.

"Because I hesitated to follow an order."

"That's only a partial explanation. Fill in the blanks before I decide five isn't going to be enough to teach you the lesson." He gave her pussy a quick slap and smiled when she moaned.

"I was worried about who might see me and that meant I didn't trust you to keep me safe…even though I didn't realize that at the time."

Damn, she was fucking perfect. She'd not only remembered the incident, it seemed as though she'd given it some thought since. "You're exactly right, love. Even if it's unintentional, that's the message you send to your Dom when you don't respond immediately to his commands, particularly in public."

Giving her swollen labia another slap, he relished the

moan he heard rumble from deep in her chest. "The swats are going to feel like fire racing over your skin, baby. But each stroke will vibrate all the way to your core and then burst into a brilliant white explosion of pleasure. By the third swat, you'll be begging, but you won't know if you want me to stop or continue." Her arousal was running in rivulets down the insides of her thighs, and it was the sexiest thing he'd ever seen.

Only a true submissive could fall so deep into a scene from the words alone, and so far, Reagan was proving herself as close to perfect as any newbie sub he'd ever had the pleasure of punishing. But something about this was different. This wasn't a carefully negotiated scene with a submissive from the club. The naked woman bent over in front of him awaiting her punishment was his—or at least he hoped she would agree to belong to him, because he wasn't sure he'd be able to let her go.

The first two swats were quick in succession and sharp enough to rock her up on her toes. Her fingers curled into the bed's coverlet. He heard a sniffle, but she didn't utter any other sound. "Very good, love. Your ass is blushing beautifully. It should be nice and hot by the time I slide my cock deep into your pussy and take my pleasure. You do not have permission to come. Don't forget that, or we'll have to begin again." Reagan's entire body stiffened, and he was sure she was wondering how in the hell she was supposed to hold back the rising tide of pleasure that was undoubtedly already barreling in on her.

Rafe was damned glad she couldn't see his satisfied smile. He fully intended to give her several earth shattering orgasms, but the first time she came on his cock, he wanted to be looking into her eyes. He landed the next swat so that his large hand almost covered her entire ass. The implements he planned to use tomorrow night wouldn't push her further than his hand. The goal wasn't to turn her away from the lifestyle. Rather he wanted Reagan to understand the freedom she'd find if she could only surrender.

"Please, sir." And there it was—the softly whispered plea he'd predicted. He wasn't going to ask her what she was begging for, because he was certain she wouldn't be able to articulate the need. He'd seen many Doms set their submissives up for failure, but that had never been his style. Asking Reagan a question he was sure she couldn't answer wouldn't do anything to build trust between them.

"We're almost there, baby. Two more and then I'm going to fuck you. As soon as I've gotten off, we're going to take a shower together." He didn't give her time to think about the implications of what he'd just said before he delivered the last two slaps, one immediately after the other. These had been harsher than the first three, and her knees buckled briefly before she moved back into position. He gave her a few seconds for the pain to morph into something much more pleasurable before he moved behind her and pushed balls deep in one thrust.

She screamed, and he felt her internal muscles clamp down around him, testing his control. For the first time since he'd been a teenager, Rafe almost lost control of his release. The combination of her submission and tight sheath threatened to launch him over the edge. He'd been so lost in the fog of desire, so eager to fuck her Rafe had forgotten her earlier admission that she hadn't had sex in a couple of years.

Without moving, he asked, "Are you okay, baby?" Her vaginal walls rippled around him and her soft groan answered his question, but he waited—needing to hear the words. "Reagan, I asked you a question and I expect an answer."

"I'm sorry, Sir. I had to pull myself together enough to respond. I'm afraid that first stretch was so amazing I almost came, and I couldn't think of anything but holding back. I'm fine, other than worrying about coming without permission, because sweet Mother of God, it feels so good."

Rafe had made subs come just by talking to them—hell, he'd done it numerous times. After all, ninety percent of the pleasure of sex originated in the brain. But he'd never had a woman's words send *him* so perilously close to the edge. Reagan's willingness to be transparent was a gift he'd treasure. Leaning down, he pressed his lips against the sensitive shell of her ear. His hoarse whisper of possession made her shiver and solidified his commitment to the truth of the one word he'd managed to push past his lips. "Mine." It was a cross between a declaration and a promise. Then he pulled back and surged forward, inching deeper with each thrust until the tip of his cock pressed against her cervix.

Knowing his seed was going to splash against the opening to her womb sent a lightning bolt of possessiveness arching through him. It wasn't until that moment that he realized he hadn't worn a condom. He'd never fucked a woman without protection, but he couldn't force himself to pull out before the first spurts of cum exploded from his balls. The heat seared its way from his tip, and the feeling of his cum washing back over his sensitive tip almost made his knees buckle out from under him.

His body lay pressed against hers. He prayed he wasn't crushing her, because there wasn't a chance in hell his arms would hold him up enough to roll to the side. Hopefully, his knees would regain some dignity, and he'd be able to stand in a few seconds.

"Fucking hell, baby. You decimated me." He'd known it would be good between them, but this was so far beyond *good* he wasn't even sure there was a word to describe it.

The walls of her pussy were rippling around him, and he was absurdly pleased when his cock remained hard. She hadn't said anything to him, but he could tell by her breathing she was struggling to hold her orgasm at bay. That knowledge fueled his effort to stand. Feeling his dick slip free of her depths was bittersweet, but seeing his pearly white seed flow from between her folds made him want to beat his chest like fucking Tarzan. *Christ, I'm turning into a God damned Neanderthal.*

An hour later, he emerged from the shower with Reagan cradled against his chest. He'd given her two screaming orgasms that left her as limp as the over-cooked noodle she'd compared herself to. He set her on the counter after toweling her off. The intimacy of combing her hair made him want to slide her to the edge of the marble surface, bury himself to the hilt, and begin all over again.

Rafe made certain she was steady on her feet before leading her to bed. Climbing in behind her, he pulled her against his chest. With his arm wrapped around her, his hand cupped her breast possessively. "I've never fucked a woman without a condom, baby. I'm sorry I didn't protect you, but I swear to you that I'm clean."

"It was a first for me, too. I'm on birth control, and I'm clean, also. I don't have a lot of experience, but I remember I hated the way latex felt inside me. You felt…well, you felt so much better. Much hotter. Sexier."

"All the more reason to for us to forgo having sex at the club. Condoms are required, even in the private rooms, and I don't want anything between us when I'm inside you." In truth, Rafe wasn't sure he'd be able to give up the intimacy of being skin to skin when he made love to Reagan. *Made love to?* Since when did he think of sex as making love?

He'd never considered sex anything but a purely physical connection—and God knew he'd *connected* with a lot of women over the years. But none of them had touched his soul the way Reagan had. Something deep inside him had recognized she was special the first time he saw her. That was the reason he'd been so hesitant to engage her. He'd instinctively recognized he'd only get one shot, and he'd made sure he was ready before asking her to dinner.

During a conversation with his father a few days earlier, Rafe had asked his dad when he'd known his mom was "the one." His dad had chuckled, but he hadn't answered right away, and Rafe appreciated him taking the time to choose his words carefully.

"I knew the first time I laid eyes on her. I'm not saying it was love at first sight, because true love takes time to develop, but I recognized my soul's response to her immediately. That probably sounds cliché, but it's the God's truth."

Their conversation had veered in another direction, but before he disconnected, his dad offered a bit of parting wisdom as he often did. "Some opportunities are only offered once, son. And it's damned hard to live with regrets." Those words replayed in his mind again as held Reagan wrapped in his arms. He'd always expected to marry someday, but for some reason, he assumed the realization that the woman he was dating was *the one* would be made over the course of months, perhaps years. And he'd certainly never expected his heart to make the decision so easily.

Feeling Reagan's body go lax in his arms, the steady rise and fall of her chest pushed her breast against his palm as if taunting him to acknowledge the truth. Rafe had never let fear hold him back, and he wasn't going to start now. *Just because you didn't see it coming doesn't mean it isn't real.*

Chapter Twenty-Four

REAGAN WASN'T SURE where Rafe had gotten the dress—personally, she considered that a very liberal use of the term—he'd given her to wear this evening at the club. Thank God, he'd given her one of his coats to wear over the nearly transparent bit of fabric or she'd have probably been arrested before they ever arrived. "You're mumbling, Peach."

"Sorry, sir, but I think the cold wind blowing up your coat might have turned my pink bits blue." As soon as the words left her mouth, Reagan suspected she'd made a mistake. She saw his eyes darken as a mischievous smile curved his lips and realized how monumental that mistake had been. *We've barely made it through the front door of the club, and I'm already in trouble. It's going to be a very long night.*

"You're mumbling again. Tell me what you just said." He'd turned to her, and the look on his face silenced any argument she might have tried. Rafe listened and his expression softened when she repeated what she'd thought had only been spoken in her head. "You're not in trouble, love. At least not in the way you're thinking. But I am planning to make sure your lovely *pink bits*, as you refer to them, haven't been irreparably harmed by Mother Nature's first winter tantrum."

She felt her face flush scarlet and wished the floor

would open up and swallow her whole. "Hand me the coat, Reagan." Without letting her gaze stray from his, she untied the belt at her waist. It was the only thing holding the coat closed since he demanded she keep it open and her dress pulled up to her waist during the short drive to the club. The car had been warm, but walking across the parking lot had seemed almost endless. "You know, if you hadn't distracted me before we left the house, we'd have arrived early enough to find a much closer place to park. If I find your bits really are blue, I'm going to insist Nate and Taz offer valet service in the future."

She could tell that he was teasing her, but that didn't stop her from shuddering at the realization he planned to inspect her right here in the club's crowded entrance. "Why do we need valet service?" Taz's voice sounded over her right shoulder, and she unconsciously looked to the floor, hoping to find that hole.

His booming laughter startled her, and she groaned at the knowledge he'd heard her thoughts. *I really do feel sorry for Kodi.*

"Don't. She holds her own just fine." Reagan barely registered when Rafe pulled the coat from her shoulders and handed it to the receptionist. Taz continued to watch her closely before finally speaking. "Now, tell me why you're hoping the floor opens up under your feet."

"I think it's my best hope for getting out of this with any dignity, Sir." *Might as well just put it out there. The rat probably already knows the truth anyway.*

Rafe's brow lifted, but she saw the light of amusement in his eyes. "Reagan is worried the frigid air blowing up her dress has turned her *pink bits* blue. I merely want to check to make sure she isn't in need of medical attention." It took every bit of control she could muster to not roll her eyes at his overly dramatic remark. *Geez, talk about hamming it up for an audience.*

"Well, I can certainly see where that would be worrisome. And possibly a liability issue for the club, as well. In that case, I think you should lift her up on the counter and have a look." Reagan stopped breathing. The counter in front of them was high. Very high. If they set her up there and ordered her to spread her legs, her pussy was going to be practically eye level for everyone standing around watching.

Before she'd finished the horror show playing so vividly in her mind, it became reality. Rafe easily lifted her onto the cold marble, making her shiver. He stepped back, the command ringing out loud and clear. "Lift your dress and spread your legs, Peach." She blinked several times, but before her gaze could move around the room, his voice centered her. "Look only at me, Reagan. I'm your Master. Therefore, I'm the only one you need to be concerned with." Those few words were all she needed to find her courage. Lifting the front of her dress to her waist...not far since it had barely been decent to begin with, she spread her legs.

"They don't look blue to me. As a matter of fact, I'd say they are actually a very lovely shade of rose."

"Nice and shiny, too. I think your sub might be a bit of an exhibitionist, Master Rafe. That's probably something you'll enjoy exploring with her." The teasing in Taz's tone wasn't lost on her, but she didn't look to see if he was smiling. Her gaze was riveted to Rafe's. She watched his eyes raise and lower as his focus shifted between her eyes and her sex. He was standing several feet in front of her, but the heat in his eyes felt like a warm caress.

"I believe you are right. And I must say, I'm relieved

she doesn't seem to be suffering from any constriction, either. Those swollen tissues indicate a nice healthy blood flow to the region." She ached to close her legs when she heard murmurs of approval around the room. Rafe turned to the man standing to his left and nodded. "I agree, she's perfect. And I'm damned lucky that she's mine."

Reagan didn't recognize the man, and even though Rafe seemed to know him, she didn't get the impression they were friends. The man's response was too quiet for her to hear, but Rafe's entire demeanor changed in an instant. He stepped forward, sheltering her from view as he turned to the man who was now grinning like a stooge. "I'll be watching, Rafe. All's fair in love and war, you know?" He walked away, but not before giving her a wink she suspected had very little to do with flirting. The man was deliberately trying to provoke Rafe, but she didn't know why.

Taz chuckled beside them. "As I recall, the two of you used to be friendlier."

"He's an ass. He's always been an ass. He is just better at hiding it during certain phases of the moon."

"I'll admit he can be snarly at times, but I'm not convinced he's a werewolf." Kodi's sweet voice came from behind her, but when Reagan started to turn, Rafe's warm hand atop her thigh kept her in place.

"You do not have permission to move. And I'd encourage you to ignore Kodi's assessment. She'd do well to steer clear of my cousin." *Cousin?* "Yes, cousin. He's been a pain in the ass since he was a kid. The only reason he's still alive is because I adore my aunt."

RAFE LIFTED REAGAN from the counter and set her on her feet. When she leaned forward to press a kiss against his cheek, his chest tightened. "I think there is a very sweet man lurking inside you, Master."

Leaning close, he kissed the sensitive spot he'd discovered behind her ear. "I hope you still feel the same way at the end of the evening, Peach." Pulling back, he took her hand. "Come." He led her into the club's main room where they met Nate standing like a sentry.

"I'd like a word with Reagan before you begin." It didn't escape Rafe's attention that the club owner hadn't asked, nor had he referred to Reagan as his submissive. *And whose fault is that? You've already been reminded once this evening that she isn't wearing a collar.*

He kissed Reagan before skimming his fingers down her arm to encircle her wrist. Lifting her hand, he kissed her palm and smiled when she turned her hand to press it against his cheek. The tenderness of her touch matched that in her eyes, and he suddenly wished they were back home, enjoying the privacy of his playroom. But he'd promised to teach her, and this part of the lifestyle he wasn't sure he could give up, so it was certainly something she needed to experience. He couldn't expect her to make an informed decision later this evening unless she'd been given at least a taste of what it would mean to belong to him.

"I'll get us something to drink. We'll begin as soon as Master Nate is satisfied you're here of your own free will." He could tell his words surprised her, and it pleased him to know she couldn't imagine anyone thinking differently. Nodding to Nate, he turned and walked away, surprised at how difficult it was to leave her in the other man's care.

When he approached the bar, Mistress Ann gave him a warm smile. "He's just doing his job, Rafe. He'll make sure she knows her safe word and when to use it. He trusts you, but as her employer, he feels a certain responsibility for her." Rafe didn't respond, because he understood, but it still chafed at his pride. In all his years as a Dom, he'd never failed to heed a safe word.

"Take it from me, it's a lot harder to process a sub's safe word when you're in love with them."

"What do you mean?" Her words struck him as completely inverse of what he'd have assumed.

"You hear better with your head than your heart, Rafe. It's much easier to become caught up in the passion when your heart is involved."

Nate stepped back from Reagan and smiled as he approached the bar. "You're good to go. Any changes I need to be aware of?"

"No." They'd spoken on the phone that afternoon; Nate and Taz both made suggestions, and he'd appreciated their input. He wanted this scene to be intense, but not overwhelming for Reagan. He hadn't worked with a newbie for a long time, and never one who'd been as traumatized as Reagan. Taz would be standing nearby to monitor what was going through her head, but he'd promised he wouldn't interfere unless her mental or physical safety was at stake.

Rafe led her to the small stage at the back of the main room, a small select group of spectators was already present. When he felt her steps falter, he stopped and turned her to face him. "Do you trust me, Reagan?"

"Yes, Sir." She hadn't hesitated, her answer filled with confidence.

"You have a safe word, but I don't intend for you to need it. The punishment you had last night was harsher than what you'll experience tonight." Because the paddle he'd chosen would spread the force out over a wider area than his hand, and tonight, the real punishment was going to be testing her boundaries. Correcting a sub's behavior didn't always involve impact play.

He wrapped his hands around her waist and lifted her up onto the stage. He heard her soft gasp when she saw the spanking bench. "Come on. I want to get your punishment out of the way, first. I have something much more enjoyable planned for later." At least he hoped she'd find it enjoyable. He was taking a huge risk, planning something so unexpected, but he wasn't about to turn back now.

"Do you know why I'm not asking you to strip, Peach?" He'd chosen a dress that would give him the access he needed, but would still give her some illusion of being covered. Tonight was about pushing boundaries, not shattering them.

She nervously fingered the hem of her dress and nodded. When he frowned, she whispered, "They're going to be able to see everything anyway, because this dress is so short."

"Yes, it is and it has a special feature I don't believe you've noticed yet." He pulled a small set of nipple clamps from his pocket and held them out for her to see. Her chocolate colored eyes went wide but she didn't make a sound until he reached between the folds of the dress. When he found the slit she hadn't noticed, he pushed the fabric apart, baring her breasts to his view.

Rolling first one nipple and then the other between his

fingers, he had the clamps on within seconds. Damn, he loved how responsive she was to his touch. The clamps he'd chosen were mild by anyone's standards, but they'd be enough to distract her while he moved her into position. She was quivering by the time he'd secured the last of the restraints, and he grinned when he ran his fingers through the drenched folds of her sex.

Turning to the audience, he announced. "My lovely submissive didn't believe she would enjoy being bare to your view." Holding up his soaked fingers, he added, "I think she's wrong. What do you think?" Cheers went up, along with a couple of wolf whistles, which he suspected were from her friends rather than their Masters.

He'd chosen a large, round paddle. The slaps would sound vicious, but the pain would be negligible. Squatting down so he could look into her eyes, his heart stuttered when he saw tears already pooling in their terrified depths. "Reagan, you have a safe word. Do you want to use it?" He hoped she wouldn't because he was sure she would always regret not taking this chance. But the choice had to be hers, and he waited patiently while she pulled herself together.

"No, Sir. I'm fine. Seeing your face helps."

For the first time since he'd become a Dom, Rafe dreaded a punishment. Not because she hadn't earned it—she certainly had. But because his heart wanted to do something else entirely. Mistress Ann's words replayed in his ears, and he made a mental note to thank her later for her wisdom.

"Ten swats. I want you to remember this. I'd have much preferred you'd been out of position when I arrived and had taken the time to retrieve your phone." When she nodded, he grinned. "You'll make a better choice next time. Do not come until I give you permission." The look she gave him would earn her additional swats later in their relationship, but today, it made him laugh. "You were already drenched, baby. Trust me when I tell you, holding back your orgasm is going to be harder than enduring the slaps against your very fine ass."

After a brief, vague explanation to the audience, he raised the paddle and landed the first swat. He hadn't warned her because he didn't want her to tense up. Her anticipation of the pain would have been far worse than reality. Rafe heard her gasp, but she didn't make another sound. "Don't concern yourself with the count, baby. That's my job. I want you to focus on how your body *feels*, not the way you *think* it should feel."

By the time he was almost finished, he could see her juices running down the insides of her thighs. The paddle had a lovely wet spot, and he was considering framing it. He'd love to hang in in his playroom as a memento of his sub's first public scene. Maybe a nice engraved gold placard to make sure they never forgot the occasion or date. Reagan's ass was hot pink, but her soft gasping breaths and the way her body strained upward in anticipation, telling him she wasn't in any real pain.

Moving to once again squat down in front of her, Rafe was thrilled to see her eyes glazed over with desire. She was battling valiantly to hold back her release, and if her panting breaths were any indication, she was awfully close to losing the battle. "Two more, Peach. After the second one, I'll give you the command to come." He didn't wait for her to acknowledge his words, even though he probably should have. For the first time ever, Rafe was out of patience. All he could think about was giving her the release she so desperately needed and finishing the scene.

The ninth swat was much harsher than the previous

eight, and he knew she'd felt the difference when she screamed, "Please." Her ass might feel like it was on fire, but her body was no longer able to distinguish between pleasure and pain.

He let her thoughts tumble over for several seconds as he caressed the fiery cheeks of her ass. The gush of her sweet syrup when he slid his fingers between her swollen folds told him she was teetering on the edge of a cataclysmic orgasm. It probably should embarrass him realizing how much pleasure he gained from that knowledge, but all he could think about was shoving himself balls deep and send them both into oblivion.

Letting the paddle clatter to the floor, Rafe slapped his hand directly atop her sex and growled against her ear, "Come for me, Peach." Plunging his fingers into her slick heat, he had no trouble finding her sweet spot. Her vaginal walls were already gripping him with a strength that made him nearly come in his damned pants. With one firm press against her G-spot, Reagan flew directly into a second, even stronger, orgasm. Using her natural lubrication, he circles her anus several times before pushing inside.

The penetration sent her over a third time, this one more intense than the previous two. Her body glistened under the lights from the sheen of sweat, and he'd need to make certain she was properly cooled down and dry before bundling her into his car. *It's going to be a record breaking trip up the mountain. I hope Brandt Morgan isn't anywhere around.*

When she'd settled, he released her from the restraints and helped her kneel. He'd loosened the tension on the clips twice during their scene, so removing them caused her very little discomfort. "I'll kiss your tender nipples when we get home, baby, and I promise you'll forget all about the clamps."

Standing in front of her, Rafe pulled a long, slender black velvet box from his pocket. When he flipped the lid open, he saw her eyes widen. The etched platinum necklace was simple, but far from plain. It would sparkle when it caught the light without drawing unwanted attention when she was out in public. "Do you know what this is, Peach?

"Yes. Well, I think I do, Master." Hearing her automatically switch to the honorific he preferred convinced him that he'd made the right decision.

"We'll work out all the details later, but I didn't want to wait another minute before making you mine." Tears streamed down her face, and he was pleased she kept her eyes on him rather than on the gift she was about to receive. "Do you want to be mine, Reagan?"

"Yes. Yes, please. I already belong to you, Master"

His heart clenched as he snapped the locking mechanism into place and placed the chain holding the only key over his head. "And now, everyone will know that you are mine. And that I am yours." Cheers erupted around them as he helped her to her feet and wrapped her in the warm blanket Taz handed him. He held her close as they accepted congratulations, but all he could think about was getting her home and beneath him.

As the crowd slowly drifted back to the main part of the club, Nate appeared at this side. He waved toward one of the emergency exits where Taz and Kodi stood holding their coats and his toy bag. "Your car is just out back. It's all warmed up and ready to go. Congratulations, man." The big man leaned down and pressed a kiss against Reagan's forehead. "No work for a couple of days, sweetness. I'm damned proud of you. That was an incredible scene, and Kodi is going to reap the benefits as soon as we get you two out of here."

After what seemed like another endless round of congratulations and goodbyes, they were finally settled into the car. She'd winced when her ass met the heated seats, making him smile. "I'm going to kiss every inch of you when I get you home. There won't be a spot I don't lavish with love." Startled at the realization that was the first time he'd said it out loud, he looked over to see surprise in her eyes.

Pulling quickly to the side of the road, he leaned over the console and sealed his lips over hers for a long, lingering kiss that was meant to be a promise of things to come. "I do love you, Peach. Love isn't about how long you've known someone. It's the realization you can't imagine your life without them."

"I love you, too. I think I've loved you since you first called me Peach." This time it was her turn to initiate the kiss, but this one was little more than a quick press of her lips to his own. "Can we go home now?"

Sweeter words had never been spoken.

Epilogue

Six Months Later

RAFE NEWELL WATCHED his new wife pace the length of Sage Morgan's opulent office. Anyone who didn't know her would assume she was being held captive. "She looks like a caged tigress." Sage's observation was dead on.

"Pretty ironic considering the view on the other side of the glass." Sage's answering laughter proved he knew how easily distraction could obscure the view. The floor to ceiling windows framed Mother Nature in all her glory to Reagan's right. Well, make that her left now. Glancing at the man standing beside him, Rafe shook his head. "I thought the song *You Had Me From Hello* was nothing more than a cliché country music ballad before I met Reagan."

"And then you found out what the rest of us have learned over the past few years—the right woman changes everything."

Rafe nodded in agreement. Sage Morgan's remark couldn't have been any more accurate. Rafe had already been making changes in his life when he met Reagan, but she'd fast-tracked his plans in ways he could have never foreseen.

"Honestly, I thought my mother would be livid when we eloped, but two minutes alone with Reagan and she was a puddle of adoring goo." He'd expected his dad to fall in love with Reagan, but his mother's approval had come faster than he'd hoped. "The party you hosted helped tremendously."

"Never let it be said the Morgan women don't love throwing a party." Rafe laughed, because it had been easy to see how much the five Morgan wives and their mother-in-law enjoyed one another's company. "It was fascinating to sit back and watch them brainstorm how to get your mom on board."

"Using Josie was pure genius." Colt Morgan's wife, Josie—known to the world as singing sensation Josephine Alta—had issued a personal and very public invitation to his family during one of her sold out concerts. When she'd heard his parents were spending the winter in Miami, she'd sent the VIP tickets to the first of her south Florida shows. His mother, father, and sister had been treated like royalty, and Josie's televised invitation had been replayed on every major news outlet for days.

His mother and sister were instant celebrities with all their friends and were still gushing about it during their phone calls. His dad had just chuckled. "Well played, son. Well played, indeed."

"Does she know why you're here?"

Sage's question pulled him back to the moment, and he shook his head. "No. You and your dad worked so hard to get this done I didn't want to steal your thunder."

"As much as I appreciate your consideration, it wasn't necessary. Don't think for a minute our motives are altruistic. Reagan's reputation as a physician's assistant made helping her regain her license a win-win. If she's happy, you'll be happy and more likely to stay in Montana. Your clinic is already booked up two years in advance, and it's not even open yet. And that's not even mentioning the fact Ryan is already putting her on the schedule for next month."

A knock on the door behind them drew their attention away from their conversation as Sage turned to let his dad and two men Rafe hadn't met into the room. After introductions were made, Rafe led Reagan to the large leather sofa and asked her to sit while Sage and Dean Morgan introduced the first man. Montana's medical licensing board had not only issued Reagan's license in record time, they'd sent one of their legal team to personally deliver the documents.

As soon as she fully understood what the men had told her, tears of gratitude flowed down her tan cheeks. The three weeks they'd spent in the Caribbean had done wonders to heal both her body and spirit. The downtime had also given Rafe a chance to reaffirm how important it was to move his practice to the slower-paced western Montana. After Reagan's second round of hugs thanking Dean and Sage, as well as the obviously embarrassed attorney, she'd turned to the second man. "I'm sorry. I don't believe we've been introduced."

Rafe stood, motioning the other man forward. "Reagan, I'd like you to meet Walter Kenyard. He saw the film clips of Josie inviting my parent to the reception and contacted them. It appears he's been trying to track you down for close to a year."

The man stepped forward, his expression softening when he saw Reagan struggling to hide her dread. "Mrs. Newell, I'm so pleased to finally meet you. Let me assure you that you have nothing to fear from me. I'm bringing good news, not bad." After a briefly explaining Reagan's connection to his deceased client, Mr. Kenyard paused to give her a chance to process his words.

"Why didn't my dad tell me about his father? He always said his parents died while he was in college."

"His mother and the man he knew as his father were both killed in an accident during his senior year." Rafe had been shocked at the similarities between her father's experience and her own. It was a family tradition he vowed to break. "You father may not have known his step-father wasn't his biological dad, because he was adopted at a very young age. That's something you will probably never know. But I can tell you, after working with hundreds of clients, you'd be doing yourself a huge favor by giving him the benefit of the doubt."

Rafe agreed. It wasn't in her best interest to dwell on yet another perceived breach of loyalty. "Peach, don't get lost in the what-ifs of this. Hold tight to the wonderful memories of a man, who from what you've told me, loved you very much." He was relieved when she took a deep breath and nodded, but the sheen of tears made his heart clench. The only thing keeping him from pulling her into his arms and assuring her everything would be fine was knowing this was one of those rare opportunities to empower rather than comfort. He wasn't about to let it slide by.

He returned her attention to the attorney, who looked at him gratefully. "As you heard, I've been trying to catch up with you, but you've managed to stay a step ahead of me until I saw Ms. Alta speaking to your in-laws with your wedding picture on the screen behind her. The bottom line is your grandfather left you a rather substantial inheritance."

When Reagan paled, Rafe stepped to her side, urging her to sit down. She complied, but he could sense her need to resume pacing coursing close to the surface. "I'll be able to pay off my student loans?" Her question had been so softly spoken he wasn't sure the other man had heard her until his easy laughter filled the room.

"Yes, Mrs. Newell, I suspect you'll be able to do a lot of things you've only been able to dream about up until now."

TALLY COULDN'T REMEMBER the last time she was this exhausted, or maybe her sleep deprived brain was just blocking out everything but the driving need to find a horizontal surface where she could crash for a few hours. The past several days had been an emotional roller coaster. She'd been thrilled to see her husband and Master standing in their living room three days earlier. But the unexpected surprise had gone south quickly when he'd once again demanded she move back to Washington D.C. She'd tried in vain to explain why she couldn't, but her reasoning had fallen on deaf ears. Karl had stormed out the door after telling her it wasn't a request. From the open door of his rental car, he'd demanded she begin making arrangements to move while he was on his second factfinding trip to Columbia. *Hell, why didn't I know he was going back to Columbia again?*

She'd barely had time to register his arrival before he'd slammed the door and driven off into the night. After a restless few hours of sleep, she'd been called back to the hospital where she'd been for the past... Looking around for a clock, she shook her head, trying to clear the fog from her brain. Slapping her hand against the round disc to open the surgical unit's doors, Tally walked to the waiting room.

Her young patient's parents jumped to their feet when they saw her, and Tally pasted on a bright smile as she assured them their seventeen-year-old son would recover from the accident that had nearly cost him his life. The elderly woman who'd hit him was texting and hadn't seen the brightly clothed bicyclist in time to avoid him. Thankfully, he'd been wearing a helmet, or the outcome would probably have been much different.

After the third round of hugs, she quietly excused herself from the room. Stepping into the hall, she felt her eyes widen in surprise. The man standing a few feet from the door sent a surge of heat through her. A minute earlier, she would have sworn she didn't have the energy to respond to Koi's sudden appearance. "Did Kodi have her baby?" Tally knew his sister wasn't due for another couple of weeks, but it was the only reason she could think of for him to be at the hospital.

"No, *ma poupée*." Something in his expression made her go still. His eyes were dark with concern as he closed the distance between them. "Come. We need to talk before the reporters arrive." *Reporters?* He led her into a conference room at the end of the hall, since the small room was usually locked and only available to staff.

"You're scaring me." She hated how small her voice sounded, but the knot of worry in her chest was growing exponentially. And she knew the only thing keeping her feet moving one in front of the other was the adrenaline flooding her system.

"I'm sorry, sweetheart, but I didn't want you to be blindsided by the press. There's been an accident, Tally. Karl's plane went off radar a couple hours ago." She felt herself sway, but Koi had been ready. His large hands wrapped around her upper arms and pulled her into his arms. "The crash site is mountainous and will be difficult to access, so it's going to be a long wait for news, *ma poupée*."

Bone deep fatigue combined with crushing guilt washed over her like a tsunami. Tally leaned her head back and opened her mouth to speak, but the words stuck in her throat. The sensation of falling backward continued even after she'd leaned back enough to look into his eyes. It felt like falling back off the dock at the lake when she was a kid…that moment of suspended animation before the black water washed over her obliterating the sun and leaving her in the silent darkness.

The End

Books by Avery Gale

The ShadowDance Club
Katarina's Return – Book One
Jenna's Submission – Book Two
Rissa's Recovery – Book Three
Trace & Tori – Book Four
Reborn as Bree – Book Five
Red Clouds Dancing – Book Six
Perfect Picture – Book Seven

Club Isola
Capturing Callie – Book One
Healing Holly – Book Two
Claiming Abby – Book Three

Masters of the Prairie Winds Club
Out of the Storm
Saving Grace
Jen's Journey
Bound Treasure
Punishing for Pleasure
Accidental Trifecta
Missionary Position

The Wolf Pack Series
Mated – Book One
Fated Magic – Book Two
Tempted by Darkness – Book Three

The Knights of the Boardroom
Book One
Book Two
Book Three

The Morgan Brothers of Montana
Coral Hearts – Book One
Dancing with Deception – Book Two
Caged Songbird – Book Three
Game On – Book Four
Well Bred – Book Five

Mountain Mastery
Well Written
Savannah's Sentinel
Sheltering Reagan

I would love to hear from you!

Website:
www.averygalebooks.com/index.html

Facebook:
facebook.com/avery.gale.3

Twitter:
@avery_gale

Made in the USA
San Bernardino, CA
30 April 2018